LEGENDS LOST

KATHERYN SHELLY

ISBN 978-1-956696-68-4 (paperback)
ISBN 978-1-956696-69-1 (digital)

Rushmore Press LLC
1 800 460 9188
www.rushmorepress.com

Printed in the United States of America

PART ONE

CHAPTER 1

A universe away and years beyond our time, a planet with uniquely diverse kingdoms fights to stop the legends passed from elder to elder from becoming reality. This is their story.

As the day fades to night, the lights of Crystal City slowly begin to come alive. High upon the biggest hill in the kingdom sits the majestic Crystal Palace. Made from huge blocks of crystal, it houses the royal family of the kingdom: King Gerald; Queen Amelia; their daughter, Princess Arabella; and a son, Prince Matthew, who has long been away, ruling another kingdom. Eventually, Princess Arabella takes a husband and has a family.

The years have been difficult and have taken a toll on the king. He is weathered and tired from years of strife in his kingdom. The commanding form of King Gerald of the Kingdom of Crystal City stands, hands behind his back, in front of a huge window, gazing upon the outdoor lights of the evening. He is thinking about what a wonderful and interesting life he has had, and the many changes that have taken place during his rule. King Gerald saunters over to his favorite chair, nestled by the grand fireplace in the sitting room of the palace. Deep in thought, he gazes into the flames of the fire. Then he hears a noise in the distance.

Would that be giggling? Hmmm, wonders King Gerald with a smile on his face. He turns around and sees the door to the sitting room slowly open. His two precious grandchildren stand in the opening along with the wood sprites who used to play with his daughter, fluttering around in excitement. Wearing their nightclothes, the children run over to a very happy King Gerald. Smiling, the king opens his arms.

"Grampy, Grampy, would you tell us a story?" beg the excited pair. He gives them a huge bear hug, making them giggle excitedly. "Grammie said you would tell us a story before bed. Would you, please?"

"Of course! You know I am always happy to tell you a story. Let's get you to bed and all tucked in and ready for our story."

The trio leave the sitting room, with Ellie and Pooks fluttering ahead, and proceed to their room in the guest wing. Lily runs over to her princess bed on one side of the room, and Gregory climbs into his princely bed on the other side. Princess Lily's bed is adorned in pink, and there are some princess dolls on it. Prince Gregory's bed is blue and holds some of his favorite stuffed toys. Princess Lily, just a year older than her brother at the age of five, waits for her story. Ellie and Pooks flutter over to the mantle and into puffy beds made out of flower petals in little boxes. All snug, they are ready for story time. King Gerald helps tuck in Prince Gregory.

"Grampy, can you tell us again how Mummy and Daddy met? I love that story. Please?" begs an excited Lily.

"Please, Grampy! Tell us again about Mummy and Daddy!" yells Gregory.

"From the beginning, and don't leave anything out," instructs the little princess.

"My, my, you certainly love to hear that story!" King Gerald says, chuckling. "Well, here we go."

Lily and Gregory settle in and listen intently as the king begins.

As we enter the Kingdom of Hagville, we see two little boys playing in the Dreary Forest. "I see it," says Prince Elgrin and looks back at his young friend. "Do you see it, Hermie?"

"No, it's gone," replies Hermie.

The two boys keep searching for a most beautiful bluebird they have just seen. Prince Elgrin turns to look, but Hermie is right. The little bluebird is gone. They trudge through the Dreary Forest, looking high in the trees as they walk. They go deeper and deeper into the shadows of the tall, old, moss-laden trees. The forest is dark; the trees reach the dull, cloudy sky. There is a feeling of uneasiness in the air. As the boys walk and talk, they do not see a vulture looming overhead. The vulture lands on one of the tall trees.

The boys continue trying to spot the beautiful bluebird. They are amazed at it, because in the world where they live, everything is dull and dreary. They know the beautiful and colorful bluebird is special, and they must find it.

The boys hear the crunching of dead leaves under their dirty little feet. Tired of wandering in the Dreary Forest, they sit and rest on an old fallen tree. "We'd best go home, Prince. Our parents will be wondering what has happened to us," says Hermie.

"Yes, let's head back. If Mother finds out where we have been, we shall be in trouble," Prince Elgrin agrees with a giggle. They rest for a moment more and then head back to Hagville.

Prince Elgrin is not allowed far from the village of Hagville. His mother, Queen Hag, keeps a very close eye on her children. Prince Elgrin is the youngest. She forbids him to go into the Dreary Forest because there is danger in the woods.

Though nine-year-old Prince Elgrin and his friend Hermie have gone into the forest before, this time they may have strayed a bit too far from the village. The boys know they must hurry back so as not to alert their parents where they have gone. As they run, high up in a tree a vulture caws and caws. The boys hear it and are frightened by the sound, as it means they have gone too far into the Dreary Forest. They must hurry back before the queen's henchmen come looking for them.

As they scurry, they notice a strange, beautiful white light poking through the tall forest trees. While Prince Elgrin and Hermie often sneak into the forest and play, they have never gone so deep into the trees and have never seen such a light. They marvel at the sight. The light happens to be in the same area where they last saw the little bluebird. The boys are amazed at what they see and make a plan to try to find the bluebird and the light again tomorrow. But for now, they must hurry.

Prince Elgrin and Hermie make their way back to the village, where they see Queen Hag waiting for them. The vulture has already alerted the queen as to the whereabouts of her youngest son.

Queen Hag steps out of her rickety old chariot, which is pulled by humongous wild boars. The boys stop. They know they are in trouble.

The queen walks up to them. "Prince Elgrin! Hermie! What are you doing in the Dreary Forest? You know it is not safe. There are many dangers in the forest. Into the chariot, *now*!" exclaims the angry queen, pointing a long, bony finger at the chariot.

The boys hop in and sit on the dirty, puffy cushions that are on the seats. The queen's knotted red hair blows in the wind, and her dragon-skin robe flows over the chariot. She cracks the whip, striking the lead boars. They snort as they take off. They are on the way home.

The chariot arrives at the heavy timber gates at the edge of Hagville and enters the village. From below, the village almost looks like part of the forest. Huge trees are everywhere. A few animals and people wander around Soomie Swamp. When the boys look up into the trees, they can hear it, they can see it—the village of Hagville. Hagville is built of huts in the treetops, bound together by wooden walkways as far as the eye can see. Little trams hang in the branches, strategically built to avoid intruders.

Queen Hag, Prince Elgrin, and Hermie can barely hear the hustle and bustle of the activity high above the ground. Hagvillians are busy going to and from their shops. Workers are on their way home from work. All is as it should be in Hagville.

The chariot arrives at Hermie's tree home. He gets out and looks up at his hut. There his mother stands against the railing of their home.

"She doesn't look very happy," Hermie says.

CHAPTER 2

A wooden box on a rope comes down to pick up Hermie. He waits as his mother cranks a big wheel, pulling up the thick rope. Hermie goes higher and higher into the trees. Oh, he knows he is in trouble, but he cannot stop thinking about the beautiful bluebird they saw in the forest.

With a big bump and a clang, he is home. His mother stands with her hands on her shabby, dirty dress. "Into the hut this minute, Hermie!" He obeys his mother and enters their hut through a heavy wooden door.

His father, Trolby, sits on a heavy wooden chair against a huge wooden table. He does not look very pleased to see Hermie. He just points his stubby, dirty, hairy finger at Hermie, directing him to sit on a chair across the table. Hermie sheepishly pulls out the chair and sits down.

His mother, Edwina, goes over to the big rock fireplace at the end of the dining area and stirs a huge cauldron. She scurries into the kitchen, where there are big wooden counters with shelves under them. On the ceiling are huge bunches of herbs and flowers tied carefully with vines, drying. She pulls some herbs off one of the bunches. She then goes to the shelves against another wall, where there are hundreds of jars full of all kinds of nasty things. She grabs a jar labelled "Albertroken," which is a ground seed from the albertroken tree. She uses it to thicken the stew in a pot at the fire.

She grabs the jar, goes to the fireplace, and sprinkles albertroken into the stew, giving it a stir. She then takes the jar back to the kitchen.

Meanwhile, at the table, Hermie sits, awaiting his punishment. Trolby begins questioning Hermie. "Hermie, what were you boys doing in the Dreary Forest, of all places?"

"W-well ..." stammers Hermie, "we were out playing at Soomie Swamp when we saw the most beautiful little bluebird. We have never seen such a brilliant, colorful bird. Everything here is brown and black and dull and dreary, Pops. The bluebird was so pretty! He called us and wanted to play. We followed him into the Dreary Forest, and we lost him. That's when we heard Vulture and knew that we had gone too far, so we came running back. We were looking up to see Vulture when we saw it, Pops. There was ... there was a light coming from the trees. It was so bright. But we kept running out of the forest."

As Hermie finished his story, Trolby looked over at his wife. Edwina's eyes got really big and she started to shake, dropping a jar she had in her hand. She stopped and bent over to pick up the jar.

Trolby got up and went over to his wife. He put his arm around her. She said, "What are we going to do, Trolby? You know what this means. The children are in danger. We must speak to Queen Hag at once."

"Come, Hermie," said Trolby. "We are going to see King Minos and Queen Hag. We must go quickly!"

The family leave their hovel and head down the many winding wooden walkways that intertwine throughout Hagville.

"Th-there it is, Pops! The castle!" stammers an excited Hermie.

The castle stands on many trees. It is the biggest hovel in the village. It has wooden doors, round windows, and a rotting-potato smell around it. A big dragon amulet hangs above the gigantic doors, which have boar tusks as handles.

They arrive. Outside the castle doors stand the guards—two of the biggest, ugliest, hairiest, dirtiest trolls you have ever seen. They have long, greasy, brown hair full of leaves and twigs. They stand at attention and roar, "What is your business with the king and queen?"

"It is urgent business!" yells Trolby. "The children went too far into the Dreary Forest and could be in danger!"

The guards look startled and call in Crow to notify the king and queen of their visitors. The huge doors of the castle are opened by two little slave trolls dressed in chains. They motion the visitors in, their little arms pointing the way.

Trolby, Edwina, and Hermie are escorted into the castle. They stand in awe as they look around. There are huge pictures on the walls in the great entrance. There is a big, old, woven rug on the floor and a table in the middle filled with bulrushes and prickly holly. It is very impressive. Guards motion for them to take chairs and await further instruction. They sit.

CHAPTER 3

There are many doors. Hermie wonders which door the king and queen will come out of. One finally opens. Prince Elgrin stands in the doorway.

"Hermie, what are you doing here?" he asks. He glances at Edwina and Trolby, who look extremely worried.

Prince Elgrin exclaims, "Come and play with me while Father and Mother see your parents!"

Hermie looks up at his parents, and Trolby nods. The boys scurry off.

Trolby and Edwina hear whispers and turn to see who is making such chatter. There are two big gray rats in a corner, whispering about the Dreary Forest. They notice that Edwina and Trolby are watching them. They become alarmed and scurry under the big old chairs and past the table to a rickety staircase. One opens a tiny wooden door. Grumbling, they go through and slam it.

"Well …" Edwina mutters. "Apparently the whole castle knows of our troubles."

Just then they hear a creak. One of the big wooden doors opens, and a little troll with big ears comes out. He wears a dragon-skin uniform and has dirty green troll hair. The troll guard salutes the guests and motions for them to follow him into the great room. Upon entering, the troll guard announces the guests' arrival to King Minos and Queen Hag.

Edwina and Trolby bow. The couple proceeds, walking down a long rug. They pass many guards and little trolls dressed in dragon-skin uniforms lining the walkway. King Minos and Queen Hag are seated on humongous wooden thrones made of albertroken wood. The monarchs are dressed in the familiar dragon-skin cloaks.

Crow perches on the top of the queen's chair. A great, furry, black spider with a tuft of white hair on his head sits on the arm of King Minos's chair. King Minos pets his most trusted advisor, Draco. A troop of vultures lines up on a perch behind the king and queen. All are wearing tiny amulets around their necks. "Welcome Edwina. Welcome Trolby," says the king. "It has been some time since we have seen you. We assume you have been keeping well?"

"Yes, your kingship, we have been keeping well, but the events of the day have us worried," says Trolby. "Remember what happened long ago, the last time the little bluebird was seen? We lost one of our own—your very own sister!"

"Yes, my friend. I shall never forget. We must keep watch on our children as we cannot have the same fate befall them. They do not understand the danger. If they reach the end of the Dreary Forest, they could be lost forever. Once the transformation occurs, nothing will be the same. We must keep them from the Dreary Forest always," says King Minos.

"Thank you for your visit. We shall consult our advisors, and we will send for you later," says Queen Hag.

Trolby and Edwina bow and turn to leave the great room. They are led by a royal guard to the meeting area. He tells them to sit and wait while Hermie is summoned.

Edwina, still a bit shaken by what is taking place, says to Trolby in a quiet voice, "What if the prophecy comes true? What will happen, Trolby? I am so worried."

"Do not worry, my dear. King Minos and Queen Hag will do everything they can to prevent the prophecy from being fulfilled."

—◦◦◦—

Meanwhile, in the confines of Prince Elgrin's rooms, the boys sit on miniature thrones. Toy guards are lined up by the door. Prince Elgrin's rooms look like a miniature ecastle, with a great room, bedroom, hall, and bathroom. Prince Elgrin and Hermie are in deep discussion as to what they saw today. They plan to go back into the Dreary Forest to see what they can find out about the little bluebird and the bright white light.

"How are we going to go back to the Dreary Forest now?" said Hermie.

"Tomorrow, when we are at Soomie Swamp, we will make a plan and see if the little bluebird comes out to play," says the prince.

"But we must be very careful. We will wait until we see our little blue friend," suggests Hermie.

A loud clang at the door startles the boys. A guard walks in. "I have come for your friend Hermie, your highness," explains the guard.

Hermie hops off his miniature throne and winks at the prince. Prince Elgrin yells, "See you at Soomie Swamp tomorrow, Hermie!"

The guard escorts Hermie and his parents out of the castle. Trolby, Edwina, and Hermie make their way home on the long maze of walkways.

CHAPTER 4

"The prophecy has begun!" confirms Draco.

King Minos is deep in thought. "Yes!" he says. "But can we stop it?"

"There is but one way," says Draco. "If we can keep Prince Elgrin from the little bluebird until his tenth birthday, the prophecy will not be fulfilled. Then and only then can we stop the prophecy. If the prince reaches the edge of the Dreary Forest and touches the energy wall, he will be forever lost and Hagville will be no more."

"We must not alert the children," says King Minos. "But we will guard them even more as the prince's birthday nears. It is only a few more days. When the moon appears on the eve of his birthday, we will all be safe. Crow! Alert all vultures and all guards to keep a constant vigil around the prince. Let no one see or speak with Prince Elgrin until after the eve of his royal birthday. We shall also send Crow with a scroll of order to Trolby and Edwina, informing them of the royal agenda."

"Let it be so," replies the queen.

The guards stand at attention as the king and queen rise to leave the great room. The planning begins.

Edwina gathers the children at the large table for supper. Saggerella is in her room, reading her many scrolls. She is much older than Hermie, and she is studying to become a pasha—a doctor.

Their wooden front door opens and in stumbles their eldest son, Hoodly. He works at the castle as one of the boar keepers. The king and queen have been kind enough to employ Hoodly because Edwina was a childhood friend of Queen Hag.

The family gathers at the table, and Trolby spoons out their stew in silence. They begin to eat. Hoodly says, "Pops, there is something strange going on at the palace."

"What do you mean, son?" asks Trolby. He looks over at Edwina.

"Well, there were some visitors to the palace who caused quite a stir. The guards were running around, planning, and the vultures are on twenty-four-hour watch," says Hoodly.

"Oh! It is probably nothing, son. You know the queen—she likes to keep her guards on the alert," says Trolby.

"No, Pops, this is different," says Hoodly.

"Eat your stew!" says Edwina.

"Yes, Mother," replies Hoodly.

The tension is felt in the room as the family eats in silence.

Later that evening, when the children are all asleep, Trolby and Edwina go to bed. As they lie there, Edwina says, "What is going to happen, Trolby? I am frightened."

"Don't worry, my dear. The king and queen will send word as to what we are to do. Now go to sleep," says Trolby. He kisses Edwina on the forehead. They drift off to sleep.

CHAPTER 5

Day breaks, and Edwina is busy making breakfast as the children come in and sit at the large table. They are ready for their busy day ahead. Saggerella has a bag full of all her scrolls for study. Hoodly is prepared for boar grooming at the palace.

Trolby is pacing outside on the walkway. He is deep in thought. Fear of the threat to the children and to Hagville consume him.

Young Hermie enters, ready for his exciting day with the prince. The family gathers and eats breakfast. Then Hoodly and Saggerella head out for the day. The only child left at the table is Hermie. "May I go out to Soomie Swamp with Prince Elgrin, Mother?" he asks.

"Well, first you must go and feed your pet rat, Vincent," says Edwina.

"Yes, Mother," replies Hermie. He trudges off to a little hut outside.

Edwina and Trolby sit at the table, worried. A sudden caw at the window startles them. They turn to look, and there on the floor sits a royal scroll. They look at each other. Trolby crosses to the sitting room and bends to retrieve the scroll. "It is from the palace," he says.

"What does it say?" asks Edwina.

Trolby comes back to the table and sits. He takes a big breath and looks at Edwina. Then he breaks the royal dragon seal and unrolls the scroll. He leans back in his big chair and reads: "Prince Elgrin will not be able to play with Hermie today. The guards are being briefed and readied on the matter that we discussed at our last meeting. Prince Elgrin will see Hermie tomorrow."

"Trolby, you know what to do now," says Edwina.

Trolby rises with scroll in hand and walks to the fireplace. He tosses the scroll into the fire. The wax seal hisses as it burns to ashes.

"Watcha doin', Pops?" asks Hermie, coming in from the shed.

"I am just putting some wood in the fireplace for your mother," replies Trolby.

"Can I go out to Soomie Swamp now? Please?" begs Hermie.

"Yes, you may go. But Prince Elgrin will not be joining you today. He is ill," says his mother.

"He was just fine yesterday!" retorts Hermie.

"Well, he is not fine today."

"I am going to my room!" Hermie grunts in a huff.

"All right then, be off with you," replies his mother.

Hermie stomps off to his room and shuts his door. He hops onto his rumpled bed and looks out the window. High atop the village, he can see the palace where his best friend lives. *Hmmm*, he thinks as he puts his hand on his cheek and leans on the windowsill.

"I've got it!" yells Hermie. He jumps off his bed and over to his door. He opens the door very quietly and peeks out. Edwina and Trolby are still sitting at the table, quietly talking.

Hermie ever so silently sneaks into Saggerella's room. He grabs a little scroll and a charcoal stick. He turns and again checks on Trolby and Edwina. He sneaks back into his room. He sits at his table and begins to write with the charcoal. He rolls up the scroll and ties it with a piece of vine. He jumps onto his bed, crawls out his window, and makes his way to the hut again. Once inside, he goes over to a pile of straw where his brown rat, Vincent, sits. "Vincent, I need you to go to the palace and deliver this scroll to Prince Elgrin."

Vincent lets out a little squeal, and Hermie ties the scroll to his back. Vincent takes off.

Hermie quietly goes back to the hut, crawls through the window onto his bed, and waits.

Vincent is on the way to the palace, being careful not to be seen by the vultures. He hurries through the walkways, darting in and out of peoples' feet, around tree branches, and over bumps.

Vincent sees the castle and scurries past the guards and around the castle to the window of the prince. He climbs the rough pole wall. The prince is sitting on his little throne, wondering why he cannot go out to play with Hermie. He sees Vincent on the window ledge and notices little scroll on the rat's back. He runs over and unties the scroll. He gives Vincent a peanut and Vincent scurries off. Prince Elgrin goes into his bedroom and sits on his rumpled little royal bed. He opens the scroll carefully and reads the message: "*We will plan for tomorrow at Soomie Swamp.*"

Prince Elgrin smiles and puts the scroll under his mattress. He will see Hermie tomorrow, and they can plan to find the bluebird. *What a wonderful birthday present it would be for me to find the little bluebird*, thinks Prince Elgrin.

CHAPTER 6

Miles away on the edge of the Dreary Forest lies the Ruby Forest. The Ruby Forest is protected by an energy wall from all outsiders. It is a most beautiful, lush forest. The Ruby Forest is filled with very colorful birds, animals, foliage, and flowers. It surrounds the Kingdom of Crystal City.

Great white unicorns protect the Ruby Forest from outsiders seeking to breach the energy wall. They keep a vigilant watch.

Tiny wood sprites flutter around the woods, playing in the sunlight. They are waiting for Princess Arabella to come out and play, as she does every afternoon.

"Where is the princess? She has not come out to play yet?" asks a perplexed sprite named Ellie. She is the tiniest of the wood sprites.

"Let's go and find her," calls Pooks, another wood sprite.

The two sprites flutter off to find the princess. They flutter over lush green lawns and past beds filled with beautiful flowers. Darting over a water fountain, they near the Crystal Palace in all its brilliance.

The Crystal Palace sparkles in the bright sunshine. It is constructed of the most luminescent quartz crystals. The palace towers high in the blue sky. The cathedral windows are made of amber. The huge entrance doors are made of pink quartz. A large diamond-shaped amethyst crystal above each door glows, allowing visitors to enter. Marble floors line the massive foyer. Luxurious fabrics drape the pictures on the palace walls. A cathedral ceiling towers above the bouquets of flowers that adorn all the tables in the foyer.

The tiny wood sprites quickly flutter up the great marble staircase to the princess's room. They open her pink crystal door with much effort. Excitedly, they flutter into the room—only to see beautiful, golden-haired Princess Arabella sitting on the floor, crying.

"Oh no! What shall we do?" says Ellie to Pooks.

"Come on now, hurry! Let's find Queen Amelia; she will know what to do!"

The two wood sprites flutter off to find the queen. They dart down the long hall into the queen's room. As they enter, they see the beautiful glow of a fireplace burning. The walls radiate the warmth of the fire.

Queen Amelia and King Gerald are sitting on a couple of ornate high-backed chairs made from the trees in the Ruby Forest. They are playing one of their favorite games on the large table. The king and queen are laughing. The palace servants are bringing in some tea for the royal couple.

Queen Amelia looks up and sees the little wood sprites. "Oh! Come in, my dears. Is the princess all right?" she asks. The king and queen know that Ellie and Pooks are Princess Arabella's two favorite playmates.

"Queen Amelia! Queen Amelia! Something is wrong! We were waiting for Princess Arabella to come out to play. She did not come, so we came to check on her. She is in her room, Queen Amelia, and she is crying and we don't know what to do!" cry the little wood sprites. "Princess Arabella is so sad."

"Thank you, my little sprites! I shall see to my daughter at once," replies Queen Amelia. The queen rises from the table and gives King Gerald a peck on the cheek. Then she hurries to check on her daughter. "I shall be back in a moment, my dear."

The beautiful golden-haired queen, dressed in a white flowing gown, proceeds down the long crystal hall to the room of her nine-year-old daughter. She opens the pink crystal door. There, sitting on a fuzzy pink rug in the front of her glowing fireplace, is the young Princess Arabella, crying.

"Oh! My dear, whatever can be the matter?" asks her mother.

Princess Arabella looks up, still sobbing, and says, "Mommy, I am lonely. I wish I had someone to play with."

"My sweet, there is no need to be lonely. You have many playmates. You have Ellie and Pooks, and don't forget your dog, Monty. You have a lot of wood sprite and animal friends. You should not be lonely, my dear. What can I do?" asks a concerned Queen Amelia.

"Mumsy, I want a real friend. I want a human friend," replies the golden-haired princess.

"Oh my. You know that is not possible, my darling. You are the youngest child in all of Crystal City, and we were blessed by the angels above that you are here. For as you know, the spell that was cast when the energy wall was put in place did not allow for any more children in Crystal City. One day there will be more, as the prophecy says. But until then, my sweet, we must be patient. Your father and I also cannot wait until the day when more children will be born in Crystal City. The day will come soon, my dear. Would you like to go out and play with the wood sprites?" The queen wipes the tears from the princess's face and gently strokes her long, curly hair. "There, my dear. All better. Now go into the great room and give your father a big hug. You know that always makes you feel better." Queen Amelia smiles.

Princess Arabella skips off to see her father. King Gerald looks up with a smile "Here is my little beauty, come and give me a great big hug." King Gerald motions her to him.

"Hello, Father," says Princess Arabella as she wraps her tiny arms around the king's neck. She squeezes ever so tightly.

King Gerald asks, "Are you all right, my dear?"

"Yes, Father. Mumsy and I had a talk and she was right. I guess I just needed to come in and give you a big hug to make me feel better," says Princess Arabella.

The king smiles as the two wood sprites flutter just above his head. "Off to play, my dear, and have a wonderful time," says the king. Princess Arabella and the two wood sprites head for the palace grounds to play.

"Is she all right?" King Gerald asks as his wife enters the room.

"Yes, she is just lonely for a human playmate. I spoke to her of how one day she will be able to have some human friends. For now, she must indulge all of her other playmates and try to have a little fun," replies Queen Amelia.

The princess and wood sprites walk down the many marble stairs to the palace grounds. "I love it here!" exclaims the princess. "I have so many friends to play with."

Princess Arabella runs past the fountain and through the massive flower gardens. She stops. There is Sirus, her little bluebird friend, coming to perch on a beautiful white rose.

"Hello, Sirus! Are you coming out to play with me too?" asks the princess.

"Chirp! Chirp!" exclaims Sirus. That, Princess Arabella knows, is a resounding yes. They hurry off to play.

Soon they arrive at a mini palace where the princess and all of her little friends play. Princess Arabella goes into the play palace and retrieves a golden blanket. She sets it on the lush green grass with the help of Ellie, Pooks, and Sirus. "We are ready now." She plops down on the blanket, wondering what exciting adventure they will play.

"Oh look! Here comes Scrappy, her little white kitten. Mopsy and Cottontail are also on the way with their brood of three baby bunnies." Pook points at the newcomers.

"Yes, come and play. Where is Monty?" Princess Arabella asks. In the distance, she catches sight of her chocolate-colored dog coming from the Ruby Forest. "Oh, there he comes with his rubber ball in his mouth." The princess laughs. "I guess we are ready to play now."

Monty runs up and drops the ball at Princess Arabella's feet. She picks up the ball and throws it as hard as her little arm can throw. It becomes a race. Who is going to get the ball first? Ellie and Pooks are zooming to get the ball. Oh no! Here come Cleo and Monty! Monty dashes this way and that, trying to get the ball before Cleo. He does it. Ellie and Sirus collide in the air, landing on the ground as Cleo runs into them. Princess Arabella is rolling on the blanket, laughing.

"Oh, what fun!" she says to Mopsy and Cottontail. "Let's do it again!"

They continue to play all afternoon, throwing the ball and watching all the fun.

Clip-clop, clip-clop comes the sound of hooves. Prince Matthew arrives, sitting high on his white steed, looking very regal in his uniform.

"Hello, Matthew!" exclaims Princess Arabella.

"Hello, little sister."

"Would you take me for a ride?" asks the princess.

"Give me your hand and I will lift you onto my horse," says the prince. He grabs his little sister's hand and hoists her up. The prince settles his sister in the saddle, and they gallop to the Ruby Forest. They enter and gallop down the trail to Arabella's favorite spot, a clearing in the middle. They have arrived at Deer Meadow, where all the deer graze during the day.

"Can we stop here?" asks the princess.

"We sure can," says her much older brother. He is tall and has dark brown hair. He is very handsome in his uniform and cloak. He swings off the horse and helps his little sister down. The prince leads his horse to the nearest tree and ties it so it can graze and rest. Prince Matthew turns to see his sister running toward some flowers.

"Mmm … I love it here, Matthew! Look at all the pretty flowers and smell the air. It smells like the flowers. Can we bring some flowers for Mumsy? I am sure she will love them!" asks Princess Arabella.

"Would you like me to help you pick some for Mumsy?" asks the prince.

"Yes! Would you? And we can bring her a big bunch!" squeals the excited little princess.

Prince Matthew and Princess Arabella are all over Deer Meadow, picking a beautiful array of wildflowers for their mother, Queen Amelia. Suddenly the prince hears Princess Arabella calling for him. "Matthew! Matthew! Come and look at what I have found!"

Prince Matthew goes over to see. She is standing beside a very large green bush with berries on it. She has found a mulberry bush and is quite pleased with her find. "Can we pick some?"

"Yes, let's! I am sure Cook can make something good with them." says Prince Matthew. He goes to his horse, rummages in his saddlebag, and pulls out a large cloth that they can put the mulberries in. The pair pick for a very long time and have a huge pile on the cloth. They are still picking when they hear something running through the forest at great speed.

Prince Matthew looks up to see one of the unicorn guards from the energy wall running up to them. Princess Arabella stands quietly beside her brother. The unicorn comes to an abrupt stop in front of Prince Matthew.

"What is it?" asks the prince.

"There has been a breach, sir!" replies the unicorn captain of the guard. "You must come quickly!"

"All right, but I must take Princess Arabella to the palace first, and then I will be back. Wait for me," instructs Prince Matthew. He hoists the little princess upon his steed and hands the huge bouquet of wildflowers to her to hold. He ties the huge cloth around the mulberries, places it carefully in his saddlebag, and mounts his steed.

The prince and princess ride like the wind. Princess Arabella holds her flowers in one hand and the saddle with the other. Soon they can see the palace. *It won't be long now*, thinks the prince.

At the palace, Prince Matthew dismounts and helps Princess Arabella and her flowers off the horse. He takes the berries out of the saddlebag. The pair enter the palace with all their goodies for their mother.

"Mumsy! Mumsy! Look what we have picked for you!" calls the little princess as she runs to her mother. The queen smiles at her daughter and then worriedly looks up at her son.

"Where is Father? I must speak with him," says Prince Matthew.

His mother points to the great room. Without words, he kisses her on the cheek and bounds up the great marble staircase.

The queen looks down at the princess and says, "My, what beautiful flowers you have picked."

"Yes, Mumsy! They are for you. Matthew took me for a ride in the Ruby Forest, and we found them in Deer Meadow. Look what else we have picked for you! Mulberries! Taste one, Mumsy! They are so sweet and so good."

"Yes, let's have one, then. Mmm … My dear, you are absolutely right. They are delicious," replies Queen Amelia. "Why don't we go into the royal kitchen? We will put the flowers in water and give the mulberries to Cook. I am sure she will make us a special dessert for our dinner."

"Yes! Let's go!" The princess exclaims enthusiastically. They go off to find Cook in the kitchen.

———〰———

Prince Matthew nears the great room. There in front of a roaring fire sits the king. "Father!" calls Prince Matthew with urgency in his voice.

King Gerald stands. "What is it, my son?"

"The unicorn captain met me in the Ruby Forest and spoke of a breach."

"A breach? What kind of breach? You must go and find out more! Inform me as soon as you find out any information. Go now!" instructs the king.

Prince Matthew bows and heads out of the great room. He bounds through the hallway and down the great marble staircase. He bursts through the giant pink doors and leaps onto his steed.

They are off through the royal grounds, past the gardens, and into the Ruby Forest.

He finally arrives back at Deer Meadow, where the unicorn captain awaits orders from the palace. Prince Matthew comes to a halt next to him. "I am ready, Captain. Let's go."

They ride off. The prince and the captain pass grazing deer with great speed. All the little birds in the trees and all the little wood sprites flutter to get out of their way. They wonder what is going on. They continue to flutter about, playing tricks on each other, giggling, and zipping this way and that way.

The prince and the unicorn captain finally reach their destination. They have passed through the Ruby Forest and can see the energy wall.

"We must go closer, your highness—over there, where the guards wait." The unicorn captain motions.

They gallop to the other unicorn guards, who are lined up near the energy wall. They break to allow the prince and the captain to continue closer to the wall.

The energy wall is transparent, glowing white and blue. As they look through the wall, they see a great door on the other side, covered in vines and moss, is ajar. Someone has opened the portal to the energy wall. It has been closed for many, many years by decree of both kingdoms, never to open.

"What has happened? The door must be closed, for if one of the Hagvillians walks through and touches the energy wall, we could be lost forever. Keep some guards here and I shall consult my father. Thank you once again, Captain," says the prince.

The captain of the unicorn guards bows to the prince. The prince turns his horse to return to the palace and warn the king of the breach. His horse's stride is much slower now as the prince tries to plan what to do about the breach. He wonders how the breach occurred.

In the dining hall, the king and queen are seated at the table with their two children, Princess Arabella and Prince Matthew. "We have a very special dessert this evening, my dear. Our darling children have picked some wonderful mulberries for us to enjoy," Queen Amelia tells King Gerald.

"Oh my, you two have been busy this afternoon. I can hardly wait!" says the hungry king. "Son, we shall meet in the planning room after we have our special dessert."

"Yes, Father," replies Prince Matthew.

"Here it comes, Mumsy!" exclaims the very excited little princess. The royal servants bring in dishes filled with pastry, whipped cream, and mulberries.

"Oh my! Cook, you have outdone yourself! It looks absolutely fabulous," comments the king.

"Thank you, your highness." Cook bows to the royals and leaves the room.

"Oh Mumsy, this is so delicious! It is the best dessert I have ever eaten!" exclaims the princess.

"Well, my dear, perhaps I shall pick some with you one day, and we can enjoy it again."

"Oh! Would you, Mumsy? And we can have a picnic in Deer Meadow!"

"Yes, that would be a wonderful idea."

"Yes, Mumsy, it would."

They finish their tea and dessert, and King Gerald looks at Prince Matthew. The two men leave the table and proceed to the planning room. The room is enormous, with huge tables and chairs. This is where all the strategic military planning is done for the kingdom. They each take a seat. The king asks, "Matthew, what have you discovered of the breach?"

"Well, Father, I met with the unicorn captain, and he showed me the breach. The huge wooden door in the Kingdom of Hagville is open I don't understand. We have a treaty signed by the Hagvillians. Why would they want to breach the energy wall?"

"I do not know. If that portal is breached and they reach the energy wall, we are all doomed. Life as we know it will be over," replies the king.

"Remember the prophecy? A Hagvillian and a Crystillian must touch the energy wall simultaneously. Then it will slowly disappear and our kingdoms will merge. We cannot have that, Father. We can't let any Hagvillians into the Kingdom of Crystal City. It would be chaos. We cannot let that happen! We must inform the Hagvillians at once!"

"No! Do not inform them, Matthew. There is something about the prophecy that you do not know, something that I have kept hidden from you … from everyone," says King Gerald forlornly.

"What is it?"

"Well, almost ten years ago when the treaty was signed, the great wizards and seers proclaimed that the only way a breach of the energy wall could occur would be if the youngest-born royal children of these two kingdoms were to touch the wall before their tenth birthdays, on the night of a full moon. I know it sounds almost impossible for such a situation to occur, but unfortunately it is not, my son. It is only days before Princess Arabella's birthday. And the queen of Hagville has a male child born on the same day and at the same hour as our very own Arabella. If we can prevent them from knowing the prophecy and touching the energy wall before the moon comes up on the eve of their tenth birthday, our worlds will stay as they are for another peaceful ten years. It the unthinkable happens and the wall is breached, all is lost. All that we have come to know will be gone forever," King Gerald replies with great sadness in his voice.

"Father! We cannot let this happen! It is only days before the great event," says the worried Prince Matthew.

"I know. We will carry on with a magnificent birthday celebration for your sister. We cannot alarm her. We must call in all our forces and keep your sister from the great wall."

"Yes, I understand. I will call in the troops."

Prince Matthew rises from the large throne he is sitting on and bows to his father. Then he is off to summon the troops. He heads for a little room to the side of the thrones. He enters and picks up a great horn. He puts it in his mouth and blows. The sound echoes through the city. The troops will arrive within hours, and planning will begin.

As hundreds of guards arrive in their royal uniforms, their amethyst amulets begin to glow. The unicorn captain of the guard arrives first. Then the many captains of the army arrive. They file into the military planning room, which is even larger than the great room. They take their seats, row upon row. The seats are filling quickly as Prince Matthew alerts his father.

"All right, my son. I shall send for the queen and the royal seer." King Gerald summons his message carrier and writes a message on a royal scroll.

At last he places the royal amethyst wax seal on the scroll and it is ready to be delivered. He hands the scroll to one of the uniformed message carriers, and the carrier is off.

King Gerald enters the sitting room and finds his wife, Queen Amelia, seated at one of the large thrones by the fire. She is quietly talking to a lovely little bluebird named Sirus.

"Ah Sirus, my dear friend, things are not as they should be. There has been a breach."

"Chirp, chirp. Yes, my queen. All is not well. I will keep watch on the little Princess Arabella." Then Sirus is startled by the entry of the King Gerald, and he flies away to the princess.

"The troops are filling the planning room as we speak, my dear," says the king. "The royal seer is on her way. We must go."

CHAPTER 8

The sound waves carry high above Crystal City, over the Ruby Forest, until they reach Mystic Mountain.

Mystic Mountain lies on the edge of great Crystal City, surrounded by the beautiful clear blue river and the vastness of the ancient Ruby Forest. This is the home of the royal seer, Galena.

Galena has lived within this mountain for as long as the queen can remember. The entry is a magical doorway that opens into the mountain. In the safety of her magical mountain home, she sees all the happenings in the kingdom. Her trusted friend, a snowy owl called Zues, is her only company, aside from occasional visits from the wood sprites and forest trolls. Galena is a trusted friend and advisor of the royal family.

Galena's magical mountain home is made of rocks and crystals. Galena sits at her ancient amber table, gazing into her crystal orb. She sees that she is needed at the palace, and she begins to ready herself. She grabs some special herbs from jars she has placed on a great crystal shelf. She carefully puts them in a velvet bag she carries around her waist. She also puts her crystal orb into its satchel.

She goes to the fireplace and reaches above the mantle, where she taps on one of the rocks on the chimney. It opens to reveal a hidden cabinet. She pulls out one of many vials of a shimmery substance and places it in her bag. Little crystals suspend themselves in the air to light the room. Galena snuffs them out with a wave of her wand. She grabs her long purple cloak, ties it at the neck, and puts the hood on. "All right, Zues. It's time. We must be off to the palace."

Zues flies from his perch and leads the way through the magic door, down the mountain, and through the Ruby Forest, stopping every now and again so that his master can catch up.

"Okay, my dear Zues, let us keep on. We shall soon be at the palace."

"I am ready. Shall we go?" says Queen Amelia.

King Gerald and Queen Amelia walk down a long marble hall lined with tables and pictures. The royal couple come to the end and enter the double doors. They hear loud chatter among the guards.

The king and queen enter the planning room. The guards stand and bow. All is now silent. The royal couple proceed, walking past the many uniformed guards to the end of the room. They turn and sit on their thrones. King Gerald raises his hand, informing the guards to be seated. Prince Matthew soon arrives, walking past the seated guards and taking his place beside the king and queen.

A few moments later, the door is opened and a guard announces that the royal seer has arrived. Galena stands in the entrance. She brings her hands out from under her purple robe to remove the hood from her head. She fixes her mane of long red hair. The guards do not look into the bright blue eyes of the seer. They fear she may have some words for them.

Galena walks toward King Gerald and Queen Amelia, her long dress flowing under her purple robe. In her hand she carries a purple velvet satchel with her crystal orb inside. Galena stands before the king and queen and bows. "Good evening, your highnesses." She bows again.

King Gerald and Queen Amelia nod in recognition, and the king speaks. "Good evening, Galena. Thank you for arriving so promptly."

Prince Matthew assists the royal seer to her position beside King Gerald and Queen Amelia. The meeting begins. Strategy has been arranged. Troops and guards file from the room. Queen Amelia turns to her most trusted friend and asks, "Galena, is there any hope of saving our daughter and Crystal City?"

Galena gazes into her crystal orb. She moves her hands around the orb and silently chants. She is startled by what she sees and lets out a gasp. "Noooo!" She quickly puts the orb into the satchel.

"What is it? What did you see?" asks the queen.

"It was nothing, your highness. I am sorry if I have startled you," replies Galena.

Queen Amelia looks into Galena's eyes and knows there is something even more wrong. She does not question the seer, for she knows in her own heart that in a few short days, things will not ever be the same in Crystal City.

CHAPTER 9

Meanwhile, excitement builds in Hagville. Prince Elgrin's birthday will soon be here. The village is all a-bustle with preparations for the extravagant celebration. The bakers are busy preparing a humongous birthday cake and many different kinds of pastries: root tarts, gooseberry pies, albertroken blossoms filled with whipped tamarind—more desserts than one can even imagine. In the enormous butcher hut, they are preparing meats for the feast: braised warthog heads, armadillo steaks, roast water buffalo, and the best of all, flame-seared buzzard. At the root hut, they are preparing roasted yams, parsnip surprise, mashed horseradish root, and much more. The excitement is growing daily.

Prince Elgrin is also filled with excitement. Finally, today he can go out to play with his friend Hermie. It has been days since he has seen his friend. Prince Elgrin jumps out of bed, puts on his royal playclothes, and runs over to the window. "Yep, what a great morning in Hagville! The clouds are out. It is gloomy and just great!" says the prince. And off he goes to find his mother, Queen Hag. He walks down the hall to the royal kitchen and asks Cook if she has seen his mother.

"No," says Cook. "Now sit down and eat your gruel."

"Okay." Prince Elgrin pulls a heavy chair from the large slab table and sits down. Cook brings him a bowl of gruel, and he eats his breakfast.

Queen Hag, a bit saddened by the events of the past few days, sits on her huge, rumpled old bed. King Minos, sitting beside her, says, "My dearest Hag, I think you should go and have a mud bath. That always makes you feel better. The healing properties of mud are always good for you."

"Yes, my dear, I think I shall," says the sad queen.

King Minos prepares to go down to breakfast with his son. Queen Hag steps into her changing area and puts on a thin dressing gown and robe. She enters the room attached to her bedroom. She opens a door, and there sits a little table with a hair pick on it. There is a big rug on the floor with a large chute off to the side. She takes off her robe and climbs, one leg at a time, into the chute. She lies down and then slides down the chute. She loves having a mud bath. She is wailing and laughing as she slides down the chute at a tremendous speed.

The queen flies out of the giant chute right into a big mud swamp. Landing with a thunderous splash, she lifts her head out of the mud and comes face-to-face with one of her wild boars. Queen Hag screams. She looks around to see all of the wild boars in her mud bath.

"Hoodly! *Hoodly*!" screams the angry Queen Hag.

"Wha-what is it, Queen Hag?" stutters a shaken Hoodly. He runs over to the mud swamp, being careful not to fully look at Queen Hag.

"What are the boars doing in my mud bath?" she screams.

"I am so sorry, Queen Hag, They got away when I was going to groom them. I have been looking for them all morning. We even checked the truffle grove and could not find them," explains Hoodly.

"Well, you have found them! Get them out of here *now*!"

"Yes, your highness."

Hoodly and his fellow groomers bow and try to get the boars out of the mud bath. They slip and slide all over the place. The poor queen gets stepped on by the boars and grows even more angry.

"That's the last one, Queen Hag!" announces Hoodly.

"See that it does not happen again, or you will be replaced."

"Yes, Queen Hag," grumbles Hoodly. He and the others take the boars to a stable below the village.

Finally, some peace and quiet. I shall just sit and soak in my mud bath. How soothing this is, taking the worries from the past days, she thinks. *I must send for the royal oracle for our meeting later with the troops of Hagville.*

As she soaks, she hears a faint little chirping sound coming from the Dreary Forest. *Hmmm … I wonder what that could be? Oh well, it is probably nothing,* thinks the queen.

She stands up in her mud bath. Whoops—she steps on a slimy twig and falls back in, headfirst. Once again, she tries to get out of the mud. Stumbling, she finally makes it. She walks over to the tram to go up to her room and put her royal gown on for the day. The tram awaits the queen's entry. She steps in and yells, "Haul me up, trolls!" as she shuts the door.

With a squeal and a clang, she is pulled higher and higher. The arms on the little trolls get weaker with every pull. At last, she reaches the top. She opens the door and gets out. She walks over to a secret door on the side of the castle and pulls a twig. It opens the door to her royal changing room. The queen quickly brushes off the dry mud and gives her hair a pick, and she is ready to get dressed. She puts on a royal gown and heads for the kitchen, where King Minos and Prince Elgrin are still having their breakfast.

"Are you feeling better after your mud bath, my dear?" asks King Minos.

"Yes, I am, thank you, Minos. Good morning, my little prince. How are you?" asks Queen Hag.

"I am good, Mother. I have finished my gruel. Now may I go to Soomie Swamp to see Hermie, please?" cries little Prince Elgrin.

"Yes, you can, but be mindful of the guards, please."

"Okay, Mother, I will," says an excited Prince Elgrin. He jumps off his chair and gives Queen Hag and King Minos each a peck on the cheek.

"Don't be late for supper!" yells King Minos as Prince Elgrin flees out the door.

"Yes, Father!" they hear. A door slams. King Minos smiles.

Oh, I can't wait to see Hermie. It seems like it has been ages. I don't know why I had to stay inside for so long, thinks Prince Elgrin. He bolts out of the castle doors, past the guards, and down the walkway to the tram.

"Good morning, Prince Elgrin!" says the tram keeper.

"Mornin', Troll. I want to go down. I am in a hurry," states the prince.

"Yes, your highness." The keeper opens the little gate on the tram. "Now hold on." The troll begins to lower the tram with a thick, heavy rope.

Squealing down from the treetops, Prince Elgrin looks out at Soomie Swamp to see if he can spot Hermie. *Clang* goes the tram as it reaches the bottom. Another royal troll opens the wooden gate and lets Prince Elgrin out. He bolts as fast as he can to Soomie Swamp to find his friend.

Prince Elgrin runs and runs. It seems to take forever to get to the swamp. He stops and tries to catch his breath while he looks around for his friend.

There he is! There is Hermie! Hermie is sitting by Soomie Swamp, throwing rocks into the water. He feels quite sad that his friend has not come out to play in many days.

Prince Elgrin yells, "Hermie!"

Hermie looks around. With a big smile on his face, he bounces up from the ground and runs over. "Prince Elgrin! You came!" exclaims Hermie as he hugs his friend.

"Mother and Father seem different since we were out in the Dreary Forest. I have been forbidden to go back into the forest."

"Mine too, but you know we have to try to go back if we want to find the beautiful bluebird and that strange light. They were going in the same direction. We need to go back to investigate," says the prince.

"I know, but how do we get there with all the guards watching us? We have to make a plan."

"We have to go back and find the little bluebird and where he lives! We could be heroes! Just think of it, Hermie!"

"Yes! We have to! Now let's draw some plans in the sand so we know what to do without the guards finding out."

The two boys run into the swamp. They gather small twigs and rocks and begin to plan. Guards are posted all around Soomie Swamp and the trees of Hagville, guarding the village above. "It will certainly be hard to fool the guards. Do you think we can, Prince Elgrin?"

"Why, of course we can. We are nine years old. We can surely fool them." The boys giggled and continue planning.

After a great deal of thinking and talking, the prince says, "Okay, remember our plan. We shall go home and have supper as usual. We must not arouse any suspicion. We will meet later. You know who to call to meet us here. I will give them some royal coins to do this for us. Then in the morning, we will continue with the plan. We will have all day to look for the bluebird. Oh, what a wonderful birthday present it will be to have the beautiful little bluebird!"

The boys scurry off to the trams. With a wave, they part.

CHAPTER 10

Finally, morning arrives. Prince Elgrin runs around his room, trying to get everything ready for their plan. He carefully puts on his shirt and pants. He runs over to his window and looks out. Today he is going to fool the guards, and he and his best friend will go into the Dreary Forest to search for the beautiful little bluebird. *Time to go down for breakfast*, thinks Prince Elgrin.

He goes into the kitchen. He sits at the table, and Cook brings him gruel and juice.

I guess that I am okay so far. No one has noticed how excited I am, thinks the prince. *Oh no, here come Father and Mother. I hope they will not notice. Parents always seem to know.* Prince Elgrin finishes his last spoonful of gruel as King Minos and Queen Hag sit at the table.

"Good morning, my son. You are early for your breakfast today," says King Minos.

"Yes, Father. I can't wait to go out and play with Hermie today. I wanted to get an early start," replies Prince Elgrin.

"Finish your gooseberry juice. It is good for you," says Queen Hag.

Taking the last slurp of gooseberry juice, the prince hops off his chair and runs over to his parents. He gives them each a kiss on the cheek. "Goodbye, Father and Mother. I am off to play."

"Have a good day, son," says the king as his son darts out the door.

"Boys these days just want to play," observes the queen.

"Oh, my dear, they are young for such a short time. Let him be," says King Minos as Cook sets his breakfast in front of him. The royal couple eat their breakfast.

CHAPTER 11

Crow flies high above the Dreary Forest, over the truffle grove and around the Moogly Marsh. There it is: the royal oracle's hovel, as dull and dreary as the rest of Hagville. The oracle lives in the tree trunk of a huge, ancient albertroken tree. As Crow reaches the door, he drops a scroll, caws, and turns back toward the castle.

A little window on the door slides open, and there appear the dark eyes of the Ebbeney Oracle. She opens the door and stoops to pick up the scroll. She breaks the royal seal on the scroll and reads it to herself. "Just as I have predicted, my pet. I have been summoned." She lets out a laugh in the darkened room of her tree trunk home. She lights another lantern and puts more wood on the fire, as she knows she will be gone for a few days.

She grabs her bones and little stones off the table. She folds up the black cloth they were on and puts them into a special bag. She goes to a cabinet and gets a couple of bunches of herbs. She puts them in another bag. She is almost ready now.

She goes into her cloakroom and retrieves a black cloak. She puts it on and ties it at the neck. She puts the hood on to cover her long, straight black hair that reaches her waist. That is why she is called the Ebbeney Oracle. She has the darkest hair and the darkest eyes of anyone else in Hagville. She has been the royal oracle for many years.

She opens the door, steps out, and puts herbs at her door so no one shall enter without permission. She looks up and hears a cawing sound. It is her raven, Sparaxis, flying just above the trees. Sparaxis lands gracefully on her shoulder. She grabs her crooked walking stick and they proceed on their journey to the castle.

As they near the village of Hagville, they hear hustle and bustle at Soomie Swamp and the activities high in the treetops in preparation for the birthday of the prince. She stands at the foot of the great tram tree. She pulls the rope for the tram to be sent down and waits. It descends with a squeal and a clank. The royal tram keeper opens the wooden door and the Ebbeney Oracle enters. She holds on to the sides as she and Sparaxis are hoisted to the castle.

The Ebbeney Oracle proceeds up the walkway to the castle doors. Guards have been waiting for her arrival. She is let into the castle and shown to a room where she can put her weary feet up after the long journey. She is brought food and tea.

The Ebbeney Oracle sits at a little table, drinking tea and resting. Sparaxis caws, and a moment later there is a knock at the door. "Enter," says the Ebbeney Oracle.

A little troll with green hair is standing at her door. He says, "King Minos and Queen Hag have summoned you to the great room. Please follow me."

"Please give me a moment to gather my things," says the Ebbeney Oracle.

The royal oracle gathers her bones and little pebbles into her bag. She puts on her cloak. Sparaxis flies over and sits on her shoulder. She is now ready. She opens the huge door and guard is waiting. "This way," says the gruff little troll.

They make their way through the long hall and down the rickety staircase to the great room. The little troll motions for the oracle to wait. The little troll enters the great room and announces that the royal oracle has arrived. Seated at their royal thrones, King Minos and Queen Hag nod to the troll. The troll turns and motions for the Ebbeney Oracle to enter.

The Ebbeney Oracle proceeds down the center aisle, past many guards and vultures, and stands before the king and queen. Sparaxis flies off her shoulder and lands on the perch beside the chair upon which she usually sits. The Ebbeney Oracle bows to the king and queen.

"King Minos, Queen Hag, you have summoned me?" asks the oracle.

"I presume you know of the prophecy," says King Minos.

"Yes, I know of it. I also know that it has begun, and you know what must be done to prevent the prophecy from coming to fruition," says the oracle.

"Yes, we must not let the wall be breached by the Hagvillians or any other kingdom," replies the king. "We must know if the prophecy will be fulfilled and if all precautions will be for naught?"

"I shall consult the higher powers," replies the oracle.

The Ebbeney Oracle turns and goes up three steps to a little old round table to the right of the king and queen. She sits and reaches into her leather bag. She retrieves the thick green cloth and lays it on the table. She brings out a large candle and lights it with her wand.

She reaches one last time into her bag and pulls out a little bundle. Inside this bundle are the stones and bones. She places the green cloth on the table and arranges the pebbles into a diamond shape. She gathers the bones in her hands and whispers some words. In an instant she drops the little bones and they fall into the center of the diamond shape. She looks at the bones and then gazes up at King Minos and Queen Hag. All is silent in the great room. The Ebbeney Oracle looks down again at the many little bones on the table.

"It is the will of the higher powers that the prophecy shall be. The prince must look deep within to choose. He will only choose in the moments before. It will be up to the will of the prince. That is all I see. If you keep the prince from seeing her before the full moon comes up on the eve of his tenth birthday, then all shall be as it is," says the Ebbeney Oracle.

"From seeing who? Who is the she you speak of?" asks the worried King Minos.

"The golden-haired one. She has great powers—powers to bewitch the little prince. Once she has entered his thoughts, he will be lost forever," replies the Ebbeney Oracle.

"Thank you, Ebbeney. You may go now." King Minos waves of his hand. He looks over at his equally worried wife.

The Ebbeney Oracle snuffs out the candle, then gathers the stones and bones. She puts them on a square of black cloth and wraps them carefully. She opens her bag and puts the precious bundle inside. She puts the candle and green cloth in also. She summons Sparaxis. He flies over and lands on her shoulder. She dons her hood and is escorted from the castle by the little green-haired toll. Once again with walking stick in hand, she waits for the clank of the tram to stop. Another tram keeper lets the royal oracle into the tram. With some squeals and clangs, the tram reaches the bottom, and the Ebbeney Oracle is let out. The keeper bows to the oracle as she sets off to her home in the forest.

The Ebbeney Oracle and her raven Sparaxis make their long journey back through the forest to her hovel at the edge of truffle grove.

—⚶—

"Minos, it appears that there is nothing that we can do!" whispers the worried Queen Hag.

King Minos waves his hand and the great room empties. The guards file out just as they came in. Now sitting in the empty great room, the king says to his wife, "There is still a chance, my dear. We must keep a constant vigil on our little prince. We must keep him from seeing her until the moon comes up tomorrow. It is only a few hours, my dearest queen. We can keep our son safe."

King Minos rises and takes the hand of Queen Hag. "Let us go. All is in place, and there is nothing we can do now but wait. We can keep him safe until then. We shall go and rest, for tomorrow is the birthday celebration and we must oversee all the preparations."

"I suppose you are right. I will try not to worry, my dear," the queen replies. They walk hand in hand to the doors of the great room. Night falls, and all is quiet in Hagville.

CHAPTER 12

As the morning rays of sunshine begin to come up over Mystic Mountain, little Sirus flutters around the palace, diving down into Queen Amelia's massive flower gardens and soaring back up into the great blue sky.

Sirus takes another dive into a huge rose bush. Hidden in this bush is Ellie, the tiniest of the wood sprites. Finally, she is tousled awake by Sirus and falls off the rose petal she is sleeping on. Quite perturbed, she shakes herself and buzzes up to see what all the fuss is about.

There on a large rose sits Sirus, chirping and chirping. Ellie flutters up to him and he chirps a good morning. "Well, good morning to you too, Sirus. But why did you wake me so early

"Chirp, chirp," says Sirus.

"Well, if you want to play so badly, why don't you go and get Princess Arabella, and I shall get Pooks and the other wood sprites," says sleepy little Ellie.

"Chirp, chirp, chirp" is heard just outside of Princess Arabella's window. Princess Arabella jumps out of bed and goes over to let Sirus in. Sirus is all aflutter, diving and dipping and chirping wildly before he lands on the princess's bedrail.

"Okay, Sirus, I will get ready and come out to play," replies the princess.

Happy now, Sirus flies out the window to go and meet Ellie, so they can spend the day playing with the princess.

Princess Arabella hurries into her royal playclothes and brushes her hair. She skips out of her room, through the long hall, down the marble staircase, through the foyer, and into the kitchen, not minding all the activities going on. She runs straight to Cook.

"Have you seen Mother, Cook?" asks the little princess.

"Yes, I have, Princess Arabella. The queen and king are meeting with some other royals today. Queen Amelia asked me to give you your breakfast so that you can go out and play," replies Cook.

"Ooooh, thank you, Cook! What is for breakfast?" asks the hungry little princess.

"I have all your favorites this fine morning: strawberries and muffins and mulberry juice," replies Cook.

"Ooh, thank you!" The princess takes her seat at the great table. She soon finishes her breakfast and bounds out of the palace. Unaware of the extra guards put on watch to protect her, she is off to play. She skips down the walk and through the gardens to her playhouse. She sees Sirus fluttering around with something in his beak. Ellie and Pooks are not far behind.

Sirus flutters just in front of the princess. "What have you brought me, Sirus?" she asks. Sirus drops his special gift. The princess bends over and picks up a twig with a leaf and a most fragrant white flower. The flower is beautiful. The princess has never smelled one like it before. "Where did you get this? It is so beautiful!"

"Chirp, chirp, I will be back," says Sirus. He is gone in a flutter.

Princess Arabella and the wood sprites continue to play, getting ever closer to the Ruby Forest.

"Look, it's Sirus!" shouts Ellie.

"He's back! But what is he carrying?" asks Pooks.

Sirus flies overhead, carrying a little vial. He tips the vial and sprinkles a magic, shimmering dust on Princess Arabella. She shimmers like the wings of her wood sprites. They giggle and wait for Sirus to land.

"Chirp, chirp!" exclaims Sirus. "It is fairy dust from my friend Galena. No one will see us go into the Ruby Forest. We can play there and no one will know."

"Oh, what fun that is going to be! I can pick some special flowers for my mumsy. She will be so happy! Thank you, Sirus," says Princess Arabella.

They scamper off into the Ruby Forest. They play hide and seek, and all the little animals and wood sprites play too. Oh, what fun they are having! They go deeper and deeper into the forest, passing through Deer Meadow. They skip and play until they wander out of the Ruby Forest and into a beautiful gardenia field. There are flowers everywhere, and the fragrance is absolutely incredible.

Princess Arabella stops and gasps in awe. "Sirus, how did you ever find this place? It is amazing!"

"Chirp, chirp, it has always been here. Gardenias only grow near the energy wall," chirps Sirus.

"They are so lovely. Let's pick a huge bouquet for Mumsy."

Princess Arabella bends over and starts to pick flowers. Ellie and Pooks play hide-and-seek among the gardenias. The other wood sprites giggle, falling over and fluttering here and there. They do not know they only have a little time before the fairy dust wears off.

CHAPTER 13

Prince Elgrin finishes his breakfast and bolts from the castle. He can hardly wait to put his plan into action. On his tram ride down to the ground, he tries to spot Hermie. *I wonder if he is there yet?* thinks Prince Elgrin. *Clunk*, the tram hits the ground, and the prince runs off to Soomie Swamp to see Hermie and implement their plan.

But where is Hermie? Prince Elgrin paces, waiting for his friend. In the distance he sees Morgo and Barney, two little boys who will be helping with the plan. He walks over to the boys and they chat, all the while looking for guards. The three boys run into a bush, and the prince and Morgo quickly change clothes. The prince stays hidden and Morgo comes out. Morgo waits for Hermie to arrive.

Morgo looks very much like the prince, so the guards will be fooled. Then the prince can continue with his adventure with Hermie.

Finally, Hermie arrives. Morgo and Hermie pretend to play. They run into the forest under the watchful eyes of the guards. The boys duck behind a tree, and Hermie and Barney switch their clothes. Morgo and Barney run out of the forest, laughing and playing, trying not to alert the guards that it is not the prince and his friend that they are watching. Prince Elgrin and Hermie will return in a few hours and switch back, and no one will know.

"What a great plan!" exclaims Hermie.

"Okay, the guards are gone. Let's go," says the prince. They scurry deeper into the forest, trying to be extra careful not to get caught. All eyes are on the fake prince. The truants begin to feel a little safer and walk slower.

"I wonder if we will see the little bluebird today," says the prince.

"I hope so," replies Hermie.

"We must go into the direction where we last saw it."

"Yes! And the light. Do you remember where it was? The bluebird flew toward it. I am so excited. I hope we can find out where the little bluebird lives," says Hermie.

"Oh, what an adventure this will be, just in time for my birthday!" exclaims the prince.

The two boys go deeper and deeper into the Dreary Forest. They stop here and there to look at a dead bug or a leaf. The adventurous pair keep trudging along, ever mindful of the queen's guards.

"Hey! Look! There is a holly bush. I should stop and pick some for Mother," comments the prince.

"Nooooo! You can't! Remember that we are not in the Dreary Forest, we are playing at Soomie Swamp! Your mother will know that we disobeyed her."

"You are right. Let's keep going."

The two boys laugh and jump over fallen trees as they go ever so far into the Dreary Forest.

"Do you think that we should turn back? There is still no sign of the little bluebird or that light we spotted last time," says Hermie.

"Well, we are getting a little too far into the forest," says the prince. He turns to look at Hermie—and that's when they see it.

"Hermie! Look! Look! There it is, there is the light. That's where the little bluebird went. That's where he lives!" exclaims the prince. "We found it! We found it! Come on, Hermie! Let's go!"

The boys make their way to the light. It seems to poke from the trees. As the two get closer, they see an outline of a door covered in moss and vines in the middle of an ancient tree. The hidden door is slightly ajar, revealing the light inside.

"Oh, look, it's a door," says Hermie. "Let's see if we can peek through!"

The boys approach the great oak doorway that divides two worlds. They glance at each other, then move some of the vines.

"You look first," suggests the prince.

"No! You look first!" urges Hermie.

The two banter back and forth as to who will look through the door first—until they hear it. The sound is very faint, but they hear it.

"It's the little bluebird!" both boys yell.

Now ever so excited, they peer together into the crack of the door. They push the door open just a wee bit.

"Wow! Can you believe this, Hermie? I have never seen anything so beautiful."

"No, neither have I. So many colors! Where is this?"

The boys decide to open the door a little further to get a better look. The great oak door creaks as it is pushed open. The boys step into the light and wait a moment for their eyes to adjust to a brightness they have never encountered before. It is spectacular.

"It's a different world, Hermie! Look how green the grass is! Why is it so bright here? Look, there really is a sun! Can you feel the warmth on your face?" asks the excited prince.

"Yes, but I thought the sun was only a legend," says Hermie.

The boys sit on the grass against a tree trunk. They cannot believe what they see. They fall asleep for a few moments in the warmth of the sun beating down on them. They are awakened by the sound of the little bluebird right before them.

"Look!" screams Hermie.

The boys go running after the bluebird. That is when Prince Elgrin and Hermie see the glittering, glowing, blue energy wall. "What is that? And what is this place?" asks Hermie.

"I don't know, but I like it. Look how the sun shines. Look how green the grass is. Why are we not allowed to come here?" wonders Prince Elgrin. "That sound, what is it?"

"It sounds like giggling," says Hermie.

"Come on! Let's go closer to that wall that looks kind of like some sort of energy," says Prince Elgrin.

They see her, playing with the little bluebird and giggling. She is a vision of beauty with long golden locks and skin as white as alabaster. She is picking flowers from a bush. The boys walk even closer to the wall.

"Chirp, chirp," Sirus alerts the princess. She is startled when she turns to see a pair of dirty little boys. They have leaves in their hair. They are the same size as she is.

"Look, Sirus! Who are they?" asks Princess Arabella.

"Chirp, chirp! I have brought them to you. You were lonely and crying and just wanted a friend, so I brought you friends," chirped Sirus.

"Oh, Sirus, I don't know. They look so different. I don't think Mother would like me to talk to them," says Princess Arabella.

The little wood sprites are very excited, for they have found more friends to play with. Ellie and Pooks flutter back and forth from the energy wall, calling the princess to come closer. The princess and her friends go closer.

"Hello! My name is Princess Arabella, but you can call me Bella if you like. What are your names?" asks the young princess.

"My name is Prince Elgrin, and this is my friend Hermie," replies the prince.

"These are my friends Ellie and Pooks." The little wood sprites giggle and bow to their new-found friends. "And this is Sirus," says Princess Arabella.

"That's the bird! That's the little bluebird we are looking for!" exclaims Hermie.

"Why are you looking for Sirus?" asks Princess Arabella.

"Well, he was at Soomie Swamp, a place in our kingdom where we play. Sirus wanted to play, so we followed him into the forest until, well, Mother's guards spotted us. Then we had to go back to Hagville."

"Hagville? What is Hagville?" asks Princess Arabella.

"That is where we live. Our hovels are built high in the treetops to avoid enemies. Our village is called Hagville," replies Prince Elgrin.

"I live in Crystal City," says Princess Arabella.

"Why do you have sun here? Where we live, it is always dull and dreary," says Prince Elgrin.

"I don't know. Everything is pretty and green and beautiful here."

"Chirp, chirp."

"Oh, I guess we must go back to the palace. I have picked Mumsy some beautiful gardenias—would you like to smell them?" asks Princess Arabella.

"Okay," reply the two boys.

She puts the bouquet close to the energy wall to see if the boys can smell it. "My birthday is tomorrow!" exclaims the princess.

"Tomorrow! My birthday is also tomorrow!" says the prince. "My parents are throwing me a huge celebration. Would you like to come?"

"Thank you, but I cannot. I too have a birthday celebration. But maybe we could meet here tomorrow? We will not get into trouble."

"We will sneak back tomorrow. We are not allowed in the Dreary Forest," replies Prince Elgrin.

"We have to go, Prince Elgrin. They will be looking for us, and you know how angry our parents will be!" says Hermie.

"Goodbye, Princess Arabella!" yell the boys as they leave. They are filled with smiles.

"Goodbye!" yells the princess from a distance.

The boys make their way back to the open door. They squeeze through the opening and slowly trudge homeward. They talk about the wonderful world they have just seen. The sunlight and green grass and flowers were absolutely incredible. They are amazed.

Hermie stumbles and falls over a tree branch. He giggles, stands up, brushes his pants off, and carries on. They excitedly continue speaking about the new friends they have just met.

"We cannot tell anyone of this new world we have seen," says Hermie. "Come on. We are almost there. We must find Morgo and Barney and change back before the guards notice."

They sneak through the forest. The boys can see the guards by Soomie Swamp, watching the imposters playing and running toward the forest. They duck behind a tree and quickly change clothes with Prince Elgrin and Hermie. Prince Elgrin gives the boys a handful of coins, and they run off.

Prince Elgrin and Hermie go on to Soomie Swamp and play. The guard motions to the prince that it is time to go back to the castle. Prince Elgrin looks over at Hermie and grins. "See you tomorrow at the party, Hermie!"

"See you tomorrow, Prince!" yells Hermie as he runs off to the tram.

Prince Elgrin heads for the palace tram. The tram keeper opens the little wooden door and signals for the pull upward.

As the prince is being pulled up, he can't stop thinking of the great adventure he has had and the beautiful new friend he has met. He can't wait to see her again tomorrow. Best of all, they have the same birthday.

Clank. The tram stops. The prince gets out and goes up the walkway to the castle. He enters and heads straight for the kitchen, where Cook is preparing supper for the royal family.

"Hello, Cook. Is supper ready? I am so hungry!" exclaims the prince.

"Yes! Have a seat, Prince Elgrin. Your mother and father will be in shortly," says Cook.

Prince Elgrin steadies himself on his chair. The queen and king arrive. They seat themselves on their chairs across from the prince and sternly look at him.

"Did you have fun today, my son?" asks King Minos.

"Yes, Father. Hermie and I played in Soomie Swamp all day."

"Soomie Swamp, you say. Is that all?" asks the king.

"Yes, that is all," replies the prince.

"Interesting, because we received word that you paid two boys to play in Soomie Swamp in your clothing, Prince," says the king.

Prince Elgrin looks up with worry on his little face. He knows he has been caught. "We … well … we were at Soomie Swamp and then decided to try to find that little bluebird that we saw a few days ago. We didn't think that you would mind. We are home safe."

"Mind! You didn't think we would mind?" yells his mother. "How many times must we tell you that you were not allowed to go into the Dreary Forest? There is great danger there!"

"But Mother, there is no danger there. It is so beautiful! The sun shines, and we found a new friend. Her name is Princess Arabella," says the excited prince.

Queen Hag glares at her son and faints. King Minos fans the queen and says to the young prince, "Eat your dinner and go to your room. I have a good mind to cancel the celebration!"

"B-but Father!" stammers the young prince.

"Go! Now!" roars the king.

Prince Elgrin goes to his room, quite saddened over what had started as a great adventure. His thoughts are only of the princess and getting back to see her. He falls into his rumpled royal bed and falls asleep with thoughts of his birthday celebration and the princess. He smiles as he drifts off.

The queen finally awakens when she is doused with a glass of water. She lets out a ghastly scream.

"Now, now, my queen. Our son has gone to bed. We will post guards with him around the clock. The guards will not leave his side tomorrow. Only one more day. We can do this, my dear," says the king.

"I hope so or all is lost, Minos. Then what shall we do?" replies the queen.

"We must concentrate on the prince's celebration tomorrow. Everything is being readied as we speak. Servants and all available guards are moving stumps and tables and chairs. The decorating has already begun at Soomie Swamp. It will be a grand celebration, my dear, and we will have every available guard surround the swamp. We shall not let the prophecy come to light. Do not worry. Let us eat and go up to bed. It has been a long day," says King Minos.

CHAPTER 14

Sirus flutters around, wildly chirping.

"All right, all right, I am ready!" exclaims the princess.

"Chirp! Chirp!" says Sirus. "The fairy dust has worn off. We must hurry, or the unicorn guards will see us. Hurry, hurry!" chirps Sirus.

Princess Arabella finishes gathering her huge bouquet of flowers, and they hurry off. The troop of wood sprites, Sirus, Monty, and the princess scurry back into the Ruby Forest. As they make their way into Deer Meadow, the princess stops and says, "Wait! I need to rest a little while. My arms are getting tired carrying these flowers."

"Chirp, chirp! But Princess, we must hurry because the fairy dust has worn off," says Sirus.

"Wait here and rest, Princess. We have an idea," says an excited Ellie.

The little princess settles herself down in the grass and rests her weary arms. In a flash Ellie and Pooks return with some vines. "Hold the flowers upside down, Princess Arabella, and we will tie them and carry them for a while," says Pooks.

"All right!" exclaims the princess. She holds the bouquet upside down, and the little wood sprites tie the stems together. They leave the vine ends long. With a mighty pull, the wood sprites lift the flowers. They don't have enough strength, and the flowers slowly drift down. Sirus zooms in and grabs one of the vines in his beak.

"There, that is better! I knew we could do it!" exclaims Ellie.

The little troop heads out of the Ruby Forest. Upon arrival at the royal grounds, Princess Arabella's dog, Monty, races round and round, happy to be home. Monty jumps up on Princess Arabella and licks her cheek. She hugs him and motions for him not to tell of the wonderful adventure they have had.

They make their way through the flower gardens, past the fountain, and up the palace stairs. Monty waits at the stairs while Princess Arabella, Sirus, and the wood sprites—still holding the flowers—enter the palace. They slowly lower the flowers to the floor. Princess Arabella bends and picks up the huge bouquet of gardenias. She calls out, "Mumsy! Mumsy, where are you?"

There is no answer. The princess and her friends run off to find Cook. The palace seems too quiet. The guards are not where they usually are. Paying no mind to the goings-on in the palace, the little princess proceeds to the kitchen. "Cook! Cook! Are you here?" calls the princess.

"Princess Arabella, where have you been? Everyone is out looking for you!" scolds Cook. "And what are those? Where did you get those flowers from?"

"You mean these gardenias, Cook? Smell them. Are they not wonderful? I picked them for Mumsy. I am sure she will love them," replies the happy little princess.

"Give them to me, and I will put them in water. You have a seat. I will get you a glass of mulberry juice while you wait for your mother," says Cook.

"Okay."

Cook puts the flowers into water and places them in the center of the table. She then goes to the door and pulls a large cord. A bell is heard throughout the city.

Within moments, Queen Amelia rushes in. She runs to the little princess and gives her a great big hug. "Where have you been? We have been worried since we could not see you playing on the palace grounds."

The queen turns and startles when she sees the gardenias on the table. "Cook? Where have these flowers come from?"

"Princess Arabella picked them for you," replies Cook.

Now the queen is very alarmed and asks Princess Arabella, "Bella, where did you get these flowers?"

"Mumsy, we …" The princess hesitates, looking at her mother. "They were in the Ruby Forest. We were playing and got lost. Then we found them. Oh Mumsy, there was a whole field of them and … and I met a new friend when I was picking the flowers!"

"A new friend? Who is this new friend?" asks the worried Queen Amelia.

"His name is Prince Elgrin, and his birthday is tomorrow, just like mine. He lives in the Kingdom of Hagville, he said," says the little princess.

The queen is consumed with worry and sits down. She tries to put on a smile for her daughter, but she is so worried she just cannot. She takes a moment to ponder and finally says, "Okay, my dear. Drink your juice. Cook is going to bring you some dinner."

Cook brings in dinner, and a very hungry Princess Arabella eats it.

"You have had quite a day, Bella. When you finish your dinner, you can go up to your room and play a while before bed. Your father and I will be up to see you in a little while," her mother says. She stands and goes around the table and gives her daughter a kiss on the cheek.

"Thank you, Mumsy! I will."

Queen Amelia leaves the room to find King Gerald. The princess finishes her dinner and scampers up to her room.

Queen Amelia finds King Gerald and Prince Matthew in the planning room. The startled pair look up as the doors swing open. "What is wrong? What has happened? You look worried."

"Oh Gerald, I fear it may be too late to stop the prophecy! Our little Princess Bella was in the Ruby Forest today. She went out with Sirus and the wood sprites and found the gardenia meadow at the edge of the energy wall and ..." says a teary-eyed Queen Amelia.

"How in the world did she get that far without being seen by anyone? Not even the unicorn guards noticed her?" asks King Gerald.

"I am not certain, but I am certain of this—she said she has met a new friend."

"A new friend! What new friend? Who is this new friend?"

"Arabella spoke of meeting a boy. And that his birthday is the same day as hers, tomorrow! The name of the boy is Prince Elgrin. He lives in the Kingdom of Hagville!" Queen Amelia begins to sob.

"Prince Elgrin from Hagville! No, this cannot be!" exclaims King Gerald.

"The energy wall is heavily guarded. She would have been seen going into the Ruby Forest. I will check with the unicorn guards," says a very puzzled Prince Matthew. He rises and puts a hand on his mother's shoulder. "Don't worry, Mother. We will not let it happen. After the moon rises tomorrow, we will all be safe once more."

Prince Matthew leaves the planning room to meet with the unicorn guards.

"It will be all right, my dear. We just need to keep her safe for one more day and all will be well," says the equally worried King Gerald.

"But can we keep her safe? She has already met Prince Elgrin."

"Try not to worry. We will do what we can to stop the prophecy and keep our daughter safe," King Gerald says as he embraces the sobbing Queen Amelia.

Prince Matthew gets on his trusty steed and rides off into the Ruby Forest to find the unicorn guards. He passes through Deer Meadow and continues until he reaches the field of gardenias. Beyond the field, the prince can see the unicorn guards. *I do not understand how they didn't see Princess Arabella here in the field, picking flowers,* thinks Prince Matthew.

"Is there something wrong, your highness?"

"There most certainly is! The princess said that she was here today—in fact, she has picked a huge bouquet of gardenias for the queen. Did anyone see her? Did you see anything unusual here today?"

"I have had no reports of trespassers of any kind, sir. We spent much of our time today at the other end of the wall, but we made passes every hour by the gardenia field and saw no one."

Prince Matthew proceeds to inform the unicorn guards of all the events of the day. The unicorn guards are amazed that none of them saw anything. There would be no way to miss the princess picking a huge bouquet. It would take time.

"We will have to double the patrols for a few days until after the celebration and full moon. We need to make sure our kingdom and Princess Arabella are safe until then. We cannot afford for the prophecy to come true!"

"Yes, Prince Matthew. It will be done," says the captain of the unicorn guards. He bows and gallops back to the energy wall to meet with the rest of the troops.

Prince Matthew rides to the palace to inform the king and the queen of his conversation with the unicorn guards. He gives his horse to the stable keeper to put inside for the night and heads up to the palace. He slows his stride, breathing the night air deep into his lungs. It is so fresh and so pure. Looking up, he sees the beauty of the stars and just stands to gaze at the wonderful world that he has come to know.

"Could this be the end of all we know? Will our world change drastically with the merging of our worlds?" Prince Matthew ponders out loud.

"I hope not, son," says King Gerald.

Prince Matthew jumps, startled. "Father! What are you doing out here?"

"The same as you, my son: breathing in the night air and looking into the night sky wondering what will happen by the crest of the full moon tomorrow."

"What is that racket?"

"Oh! Yes, I almost forgot. It is Arabella's big birthday celebration tomorrow, and the crews are starting the setup. At least we can keep her busy and keep her from going to the energy wall," says the king.

They see many servants busily setting up white tables and chairs and tents for food and dance. King Gerald and Prince Matthew sit down in the grass to watch them for what seems like hours. Staff bring big barbecue ovens out and fill the tents with very long, large tables for food.

"It is going to be a grand celebration, the likes of which Crystal City has never seen," King Gerald says proudly. "And you, my son, will turn twenty-one in a few months. It is time for you to choose a bride."

"Oh Father, we must get through tomorrow. I must protect my sister before I even think of choosing a bride!"

"Let's go in now. It is late, and we must get some rest. Tomorrow is a big day for all of us," says King Gerald. The two stand and go inside the palace. "Good night, my son."

"Good night, Father," says Prince Matthew as he puts a hand on his father's shoulder. With smiles, the prince and king part ways to go to their rooms for some required rest.

CHAPTER 15

Morning arrives early at Hermie's house. Hermie hears all the hustle and bustle in the kitchen. He lies in his rumpled little bed, looking out his window.

"Hermie! Hermie! Get up! It is time for breakfast," yells Saggerella.

"All right, all right, I am coming," retorts Hermie.

Hermie lets out a great big yawn, then stretches a great big stretch, mimicking his pet rat Vincent. He bounds out of bed with a giggle. He puts on clothes and heads off to the kitchen.

The whole family is seated at the big slab table and are eating their gruel. Hermie takes his seat and eats his breakfast. They finish breakfast.

"Hermie, I want you to go with your sister for a little while and help her bring food down to Soomie Swamp," says his mother, Edwina.

"Do I have to?" groans Hermie.

"Yes! You have to. Now hurry and finish getting ready."

Hoodly is headed to the castle to groom Queen Hag's boars. Saggerella is off to Hagville to the bake center. She will help with the baking and get things over to Soomie Swamp for Prince Elgrin's celebration this afternoon.

Trolby and Edwina are also off to help prepare for the celebration. People everywhere are bringing tables, chairs, and huts, ready for the great celebration. There are many servants bringing food down the trams. It is very chaotic. Hagvillians are in the Dreary Forest, picking holly for the tables. Hustle and bustle is everywhere. Vultures and troll guards are also everywhere, making sure things are as they should be. Guards are posted all around Soomie Swamp. Vultures patrol overhead.

Prince Elgrin stands at his window, looking out at all the commotion. It is grand to watch from his room. The activity is everywhere. All the little shops are bustling. A steady stream of people carrying food, presents, and holly go down the trams to Soomie Swamp.

I can't wait for my party! thinks Prince Elgrin. *How will we sneak away to see Princess Arabella? I will have to wait till the party and speak with Hermie to make a plan. There will be so many people there. I am sure we can sneak away. I am so excited to see Princess Arabella. I hope she will be able to get away. We will have to wait until the celebration is in full swing. Then Hermie and I shall make a run for it. Hmmmm, but there are so many guards around Soomie Swamp …*

"Prince Elgrin!" yells one of the servants. "Prince Elgrin, it is time for your breakfast. King Minos and Queen Hag await your arrival downstairs."

"Okay, I will be right there. Thank you," replies Prince Elgrin.

The prince opens his big door and heads to the kitchen, down the rickety stairs and past two gossiping rats in the entryway.

"Good morning, son, and happy birthday!" sing the proud king and queen. King Minos and Queen Hag rise and give him a great big hug.

"Thank you, Mother and Father. I can't wait for the big celebration later!" exclaims the excited little prince.

"Yes, it shall be a grand celebration. We have posted many extra guards around Soomie Swamp for your protection. So you will not be able to sneak into the Dreary Forest today. We do not want you in danger on your birthday," lectures his worried father.

"We even have a special guard for you and another for Hermie, so we can keep an eye on you boys today," says Queen Hag.

"But ... but a guard for me ... and ... and Hermie! Mother, we will be at the celebration," groans the worried Prince Elgrin. The planning will be harder than he thought, but Prince Elgrin knows that they will do it.

They go into the dining room, and Prince Elgrin eagerly awaits his birthday breakfast, as Cook always makes him something extra special. "Ooooh! Here she comes!" exclaims the hungry little prince. Cook enters the dining room with a big tray of all the prince's favorite breakfast foods: scrambled buzzard eggs, dewberry cakes, holly berry juice, sliced water buffalo, and gruel. Prince Elgrin's eyes are wide and his mouth begins to water. "Yes, what a grand day it will be, starting with all my favorites!" yells the prince.

The royals enjoy their breakfast and then disperse to check on the status of the decorating, cooking, and serving. Prince Elgrin goes up to his room to watch and try to make a plan, as he is not allowed to leave the castle until his party.

CHAPTER 16

"Chirp! Chirp!" *Tap, tap, tap.*

Princess Arabella stirs.

"Chirp! Chirp!" *Tap, tap, tap.*

The princess slowly opens her sleepy eyes. Her eyes get very wide, and she has the biggest smile on her face.

"Sirus!" she says in her groggy little voice. She yawns, puts her arms high over her head, and has a great big stretch. She just lies there for a moment, then throws the covers off and slowly rises. She trudges over to the window. Still smiling, she opens the window and lets Sirus in. Sirus wildly flies around her room and chirps. He is very excited.

"Chirp! Look out the window, Princess! Everyone is preparing for your royal birthday celebration," chirps Sirus.

Princess Arabella turns to look out her bedroom window. "Wow! Look at all the pretty tents and tables, Sirus! It is going to be beautiful." Now very awake and very excited, she scampers around her room and begins to dress. "I must go out and see everything. Oh! Sirus, I just can't wait!" she exclaims. "But how will I get to see the prince today? I have to go to see my special new friend. But how, Sirus?"

"Chirp, chirp. Don't worry, Princess Arabella, I will help you!" chirps Sirus as he flies out of the window.

Princess Arabella finishes dressing and makes her way down the hall, passing many servants gathering tablecloths from many linen closets. She scampers to and fro to get to the great marble staircase. She slowly walks down the stairs, holding the railing tightly, deep in thought.

Princess Arabella bounds off the last stair and skips to the royal dining room for her birthday breakfast. Once she is in the dining room, the hustle and bustle of palace activity stops. She goes over to the grand table and sits down. Gazing upon the beautiful gardenia bouquet she picked, Princess Arabella remembers the events of the day before and smiles. She is startled by King Gerald, Queen Amelia, and Prince Matthew entering from the kitchen, singing "Happy Birthday." They are followed by Cook and her birthday breakfast.

"Oh! Thank you, Mumsy, Father, and you too, Matthew!" Princess Arabella giggles. The royal family files past the little princess. Each person gives her a birthday hug and kiss on the cheek. Cook places breakfast on the table.

"Cook has prepared a special birthday breakfast for you," says handsome Prince Matthew.

Princess Arabella looks at the table and sees angel cakes, yogurt, all kinds of berries, melons, and a tall pitcher of mulberry juice lining the table.

"Shall we eat breakfast now, my dear birthday girl?" asks her mother.

"Oooh yes!" exclaims the excited princess.

The royal family happily sit and eat their breakfast.

"May I go and see the preparations after breakfast, Father?" asks the princess.

"I am sorry, my dear, but you will have to watch from inside the palace until the preparations are ready. You need to get ready for your special day. You want to be extra beautiful today, my sweet. One of the servants is drawing you a wonderful bubble bath, and another will fix your hair. We have so many things to do before the celebration to get ready," explains King Gerald.

King Gerald reaches to one of the other chairs. There is a huge box wrapped in gold paper with a beautiful pink bow on it. Queen

Amelia and Prince Matthew also retrieve presents for the birthday girl. Prince Matthew gives his sister his present first. Princess Arabella throws her arms around her brother and gives him a big hug and kiss. "Oh, thank you, Matt! May I open it?"

"Of course you may open it, silly!" replies a smiling Prince Matthew.

She pulls the bow off ever so carefully and eagerly removes the paper. She opens the box. Her eyes are wide and her smile is huge. "Mumsy! Father! Look! Matthew has bought me white shoes with big crystal flowers on them! And look, the laces have many little sparkles on them. They are magical! They sparkle like the wood sprites' wings. Oooh, Matthew, can I put them on? Please?" begs Princess Arabella.

"Of course! And you can wear them for your party later!" replies Prince Matthew.

Princess Arabella puts on her new sparkling shoes. She is just beaming as she turns to her father. King Gerald is holding a present for her. It is the biggest of all the presents. It has the biggest pink bow she has ever seen.

"Well, go ahead and open it, my dear." The king offers it with a tremendous smile on his face.

The princess is so excited that she works a little quicker to open this box. She gets the lid off and moves the tissue paper inside. Underneath it is the most beautiful beaded white dress the princess has ever seen. The top sparkles in the light from all the tiny crystals on it. Princess Arabella takes the dress from the box and gasps. There is a thick pink ribbon around the waist and panels of sheer fabric over the satin skirt of the dress. There are little pink crystals on the layers of sheer fabric. "Oh, Father, it is just like the dresses the fairies wear in the stories you tell me. I love it! I just love it! May I try it on? Please?" asks the excited princess.

"Well, you may want to wait, as you still have one more present to open, sweet one," says Queen Amelia. She then hands her daughter the last present.

Princess Arabella absolutely cannot contain her excitement. She puts the dress back in the box and takes the present from her mother. She opens the lid carefully and lets out a little giggle before running over to give her mother, father, and brother the biggest hugs ever. "Thank you! Thank you! This is the best birthday ever!" squeals the princess.

She runs back to the open box and removes the contents. First, she pulls out a beautiful little tiara. A large pink stone and hundreds of smaller crystals cover this miniature version of the queen's tiara.

"You are not done yet! There is something else inside, my dear," says Queen Amelia.

Princess Arabella puts her little hand in once more and lets out a giggle. She pulls out a small crystal wand, also with a pink stone on top in the shape of a small star. "Oh Mumsy, may I wear it? May I wear all of them today? Please?" cries the princess.

"Yes, you may wear all of it today, but you must go up to your room for your bubble bath first Then you can put on your beautiful new dress and shoes for your grand party this afternoon."

The queen summons a servant with a flick of her hand. The servant gathers the princess's presents and proceeds out of the royal dining room and up the stairs to the princess's room. Princess Arabella takes another piece of melon from the table and announces to Cook that she is going to her room to get ready for the party.

The rest of the royal family make their way out of the palace to see to all the arrangements. King Gerald and Queen Amelia go out to the palace grounds to oversee the setting up of tables. Prince Matthew goes to the stable to saddle his trusty steed and set out to Ruby Forest to assemble the troops. The Ruby Forest and energy wall need to be heavily guarded. No one can breach the wall before the moon comes up on this very eve. All must be ready.

Food is starting to arrive and is put onto tables under tents. Jesters and musicians are setting up under other tents. It is going to be a grand affair.

Sirus flutters around with Ellie and Pooks, watching the hustle and bustle of the servants. A large wagon pulled by four white horses arrives from the Ruby Forest, laden with thousands of flowers. Servants run over to the wagon and distribute flowers to each table. The bakery wagons arrive with breads and pastries.

The last of the bakery wagons is the most important wagon of all. It carries the birthday cake for Princess Arabella, decorated with sprinkles and flowers. It towers over the servants as they carefully move it to the tent.

More and more wagons enter. The butcher wagons bring many kinds of meats to be sliced, roasted, braised, and baked. Outdoor ovens and barbecues are ready to start cooking. Market wagons arrive filled with all kinds of fruits and vegetables, ready for placement in the tents.

A few hours pass. The royal guests arrive as heavenly aromas fill the air. Music plays and the jesters entertain the children. There is a continuous stream of arrivals; the palace grounds fill up quickly.

A horn is heard and all the guests stand at attention, facing the palace. The great palace doors open. Guards line the stairway as King Gerald, Queen Amelia, and Prince Matthew escort Princess Arabella through. The royal family take their places at the top of the stairway. The royal horns sound again, announcing the royal family and the birthday girl. The family bows as applause is heard, growing louder and louder. The royals proceed down the stairs and onto the grounds.

King Gerald announces, "Let the celebration begin!" The crowd sings "Happy Birthday" to the princess. Princess Arabella bows gracefully as guests file past, congratulating her.

The guests are then led into the tents to partake of the great feast. There is singing and laughing and playing all over the palace grounds.

The princess is seated at her own table when she sees Sirus, Ellie, and Pooks flutter toward her. She smiles a great big smile for her friends. "You came!" she shouts.

"We wouldn't miss your party for anything!" cries Pooks.

"Do you want some cake?" asks Princess Arabella. She pushes her plate to her tiny friends. Ellie and Pooks flutter down and stick their fingers in the icing. They giggle and lick it off.

"Let's go play!" announce the wood sprites.

"I wish I could see my friend Prince Elgrin," says Princess Arabella.

"Chirp! Chirp! We must wait until it grows a little darker," chirps Sirus. "Then we can sneak away to the gardenia field and see the prince."

"Okay then, let's just go and play with the jester," says Princess Arabella.

They scurry from the table and stand by the clown as he does many tricks. Sirus flies away.

CHAPTER 17

"Prince Elgrin! Price Elgrin!" the little green troll yells as he knocks on the prince's door. The troll opens the door to see the servants still helping the prince dress in his finest dragon-skin uniform and cloak. They straighten the little dragon amulet that hangs from a chain around his neck.

"There, you are ready, your royal highness," says one of the servants.

The little troll leads the prince along the hall to the rickety staircase and down to the entryway. Guards line the entryway, along with the two pesky rats who also stand to attention as the prince comes down the stairs, ready for his birthday celebration.

Queen Hag and King Minos await the little prince's arrival. They too are dressed in royal finery. The queen wears a brown velvet gown and dragon-skin cloak and the king wears a dragon-skin uniform and cloak.

The guards escort the royal family out of the castle and down the walkway. Vulture guards fly overhead to spot any impending danger. The troll tram keeper opens the tram door and the royal family get in. The tram steadily goes down with squeaks and a big clang. They soon are on the ground. Another troll lets them out.

Surrounded by troll guards, they make their way to Soomie Swamp. Prince Elgrin looks around and cannot see his best friend Hermie. They arrive at Soomie Swamp to much applause from all the guests. The guards move from the front to the rear of the royal family. The head troll announces the arrival of the royals. The guests bow and then the royal family bows. The guests cheer and sing "Happy Birthday" to the prince. Prince Elgrin smiles as he searches the large crowd for his best friend.

Finally, a faint voice yells from somewhere in the crowd, "Prince Elgrin!" It's Hermie. He squeezes past some very large guests. He runs over and hugs his friend. "Happy birthday!"

"Thank you, Hermie," says the prince. He looks over at his mother and asks, "May I go and see the tents with Hermie, Mother?"

"Yes, but stay close. There are guards surrounding the swamp," instructs Queen Hag.

"Yes, Mother," says Prince Elgrin.

The boys run off to the tents and see the massive array of food. "Let's eat!" says a hungry Hermie.

The boys heap mounds of flame-seared buzzard, root tarts, and yams on their plates. They go over to a table, jump up on a couple of stumps, and begin to eat their royal feast. A server comes to them and asks, "Would you boys like some holly berry juice?"

The two exclaim in unison, "Yes, please!?

Their glasses are filled and they continue to enjoy their meal.

Soon the boys are stuffed. "That was absolutely the best buzzard that I have ever eaten," says Hermie.

"Yes, it was delicious. And what about those tarts? So good. But we need to make a plan. I need to see the princess," says Prince Elgrin.

"But how? There are guards everywhere!" exclaims Hermie.

"We shall wait a few hours and play and enjoy the celebration. When nobody is checking, we will try to sneak into the Dreary Forest," schemes Prince Elgrin.

"Do you think that will work? Remember last time! Well, all right. Let's go and distract everyone then," says Hermie.

The two scurry off to play. The hours pass. The celebration wears on into the evening. There is much laughter and merriment at Soomie Swamp. All seems as it should be.

"Hermie, we must try to find a way into the Dreary Forest. The sun will soon begin to set and it will be dark. We must try to see my new friend before then."

"Yes, but how? Look around. There are guards everywhere," says Hermie.

Then they hear it—a little chirp from the edge of the swamp.

"Look! It is Sirus! He has come to help us!" excitedly exclaims Prince Elgrin.

"I see him. He is carrying something, but what is it?" asks Hermie.

"Well, don't just stand there. Let's go and find out. But watch to make sure the guards can't see what we are doing. I will try and get a little closer to the swamp bushes and see Sirus," says Prince Elgrin.

"Okay, now! Hurry! The guards are looking the other way!" whispers Hermie.

Prince Elgrin tries not to be seen as he hurries past the crowds of singing and dancing Hagvillians. He is almost there. Sirus flies to him, also being very careful not to be seen by the many vultures overhead. Sirus lands on Prince Elgrin's shoulder and chirps wildly in his ear.

"What is that?" the prince asks, pointing to the little vial that hangs from Sirus's neck.

"Chirp, chirp. I have come to help you see the princess. I have magic fairy dust. I will sprinkle it on the Hagvillians, and they shall be put to sleep for one hour. You can go with no fear to see the princess," chirps Sirus. He flies back into the treetops, hidden from view.

Prince Elgrin excitedly runs back to Hermie. "Sirus is going to help us!" he whispers.

"But how? How will we get past everyone, especially the guards? What about all the vultures?" asks a very worried Hermie.

"Sirus has brought magic fairy dust. He is going to sprinkle it over everyone and they will fall fast asleep for one hour. So we will have to hurry," replies the prince.

"But what if we get caught? I will stay and you go. In case they wake up, I can distract them," says Hermie.

"Thank you, Hermie. I will never forget this. You are truly my best friend." Prince Elgrin hugs his little friend.

"Here comes Sirus," says Hermie. "Quick, hide under the table so you do not get a sprinkle of the fairy dust."

Prince Elgrin dives under a table just in time as Sirus flies over the large crowd, sprinkling the fairy dust. It looks as if the sky is raining sparkles the colors of the rainbow. It is truly magnificent. The guards, the vultures, and all the Hagvillians slowly slump and fall fast asleep.

Prince Elgrin looks from under the table and sees Hermie fast asleep. He crawls out and rises. It is silent but for a few snores. "You did it, Sirus!" yells a very happy Prince Elgrin.

"Chirp, chirp. We must hurry!" chirps Sirus. He flies off.

Prince Elgrin jumps over the sleeping guards and makes his way to the edge of the Dreary Forest. He turns and looks back at Hermie. Then he sees—her, someone who was not at Soomie Swamp, and he knows that he has been spotted. He must hurry, for he only has one hour to get to the wall.

He runs quickly, following Sirus. He jumps over fallen trees, remembering his trail from the other day. He is breathing heavily and sits down for a moment. Sirus lands on the long moss-covered log that the prince is sitting on.

"Chirp, chirp. The secret door is just over there. I must go now," chirps Sirus.

"Wait, Sirus!" yells the prince. But the little bluebird flies off.

CHAPTER 18

There is much merriment at the Crystal Palace as the festivities carry on throughout the afternoon and into the evening. The large tents are refilled with food and beverages. Servants gather used plates and glasses. The music still plays loudly, with people dancing and older children playing and singing. Guards are posted all around the palace grounds and along the Ruby Forest, watching and waiting. It is only a few hours before the moon rises. All is well for now.

Away from the huge crowds, Princess Arabella lies on the grass, giggling as Monty licks her face. Ellie and Pooks flutter overhead. She sits up and looks around and exclaims, "Where is Sirus? I have not seen him all day!"

"No need to worry, Princess. He will be here soon," says Pooks.

"Pooks, I must try to see my new friend, Prince Elgrin. I must see him today. We promised."

"Chirp, chirp" is heard by the princess and her little friends.

"Sirus, where are you? Is that you?" asks the startled princess.

"Chirp, chirp. I have come to help you to see your friend," announces Sirus.

"Did you bring some magic fairy dust, like last time?"

"Chirp, chirp, yes. Are you ready, Princess?"

"Ooh yes! Let's go! I can't wait to see my new friend," replies Princess Arabella.

Sirus sprinkles a little fairy dust on the princess. She is very excited as the shimmering dust falls upon her golden locks.

"Chirp, chirp, there! You're ready. No one will be able to see you for one hour," chirps Sirus.

"Yippee! Let's go then!" yells Princess Arabella.

They trudge along through the Ruby Forest. The princess stops and picks some mulberries, her absolute favorite snack. They carry on, going through Deer Meadow, skipping over wild mushrooms and mint leaves.

"Chirp, chirp! We must hurry, Princess. You must be back at the palace before it grows dark."

They continue to the gardenia field. The princess stands in the middle of the most beautiful, fragrant field she has ever seen. "Oh, good. He is not here yet," she says. She bends over and picks some flowers. Tired, she sits on the grass, smelling the gardenias and waiting for her new friend.

CHAPTER 19

Meanwhile, high up on Mystic Mountain, Galena the royal seer puts her crystal orb back onto her table. Her fire roars, heating up her home. She has some worry about the prophecy; she knows that it may come to pass.

She reaches into her bag and pulls out the little vial she took with her. She rises and goes to the fireplace. She taps one of the stones above the fireplace, and a rock door opens. She places the vial inside, then gasps as she notices that one is missing. She taps the stone. The door closes, and she promptly returns to the table.

She closes her eyes and rubs the crystal orb. She looks into the almighty seeing orb and is shocked at what she sees. First, she sees the princess in the gardenia field, sitting and smelling the flowers. Galena knows that Princess Arabella is supposed to be at her birthday celebration. *How did the princess get past all of the guests and the guards?* she wonders.

She once again rubs the crystal orb and is shocked. She sees Sirus with her missing vial.

"Oh no! I must alert King Gerald and Queen Amelia at once! This cannot happen!" says Galena.

Galena goes to an old desk. She pulls out a grand chair and sits. She reaches into a little drawer and retrieves a scroll. Galena begins to write a warning to be delivered to King Gerald and Queen Amelia. She seals the scroll with purple wax in the shape of her trusted great white snowy owl.

Galena immediately summons Zues. He arrives through the magic portal in the side of the mountain. Galena gives the scroll to Zues with the instruction to hurry and deliver the scroll to the palace. It is a matter of great urgency.

Zues flies off through the portal to deliver to scroll. Galena goes back to the table and sits down. She once again closes her eyes and rubs the crystal orb. She is once again shocked at what she sees.

In the orb, Prince Elgrin is running through the Dreary Forest. He is getting closer to the magic doorway that will lead him to the energy wall and Princess Arabella.

Galena stands and walks over to her window. She looks into the sky. The sun is low, very low. It will soon be time—the time when the full moon will be in sight.

Will there be time to stop them? wonders Galena. She sits and waits for Zues to return.

CHAPTER 20

King Gerald and Queen Amelia sit at a table, overseeing all of the festivities. The guests are having a wonderful time at the grand celebration.

King Gerald sees Zues flying overhead. He looks worriedly at Queen Amelia. "It's Zues!" he says.

"But why would Zues be coming here today? Unless … there could be something drastically wrong!" exclaims Queen Amelia.

Zues flies over the royal celebration and straight to the royal table where King Gerald and Queen Amelia are seated. Zues drops the scroll onto the royal table and flies off.

The king quickly grabs the scroll, breaks the seal, and reads the message from Galena.

"What is it, Gerald?" asks the worried queen.

"Princess Arabella is in the gardenia field, waiting to meet her special friend We must hurry to stop her!" whispers King Gerald.

The king rises and heads over to Prince Matthew, who is in the middle of a group of many maidens seeking his attention. Prince Matthew sees his father's quick stride and knows there is a problem. Prince Matthew excuses himself and meets the king by a huge fountain. "What is it, Father?"

"It is Arabella. I have just received word from Galena that she is in the gardenia field!" says King Gerald.

"But how? She is surrounded by guards. How could she go without being spotted?" asks Prince Matthew.

"Someone has stolen some magic fairy dust from Galena—that is how Princess Arabella was able to sneak away without being spotted. We must hurry and get to her before night falls and the moon rises," says the king.

"I will send for the horses, Father."

"Your mother will also be riding with us."

"Yes, I will hurry. Meet me at the royal stables."

"Okay, son. I will get your mother, and we will not alert the guests," replies King Gerald.

The king walks back to the queen. He bends and whispers something in her ear. Queen Amelia looks alarmed. She stands and leaves her guests. King Gerald takes her by the hand as if going for a stroll to the flower gardens. Instead he leads her to the royal stables, where Prince Matthew has the horses ready.

Prince Matthew helps his mother onto her royal steed. Prince Matthew and King Gerald mount their horses, and they are off. All the guards are on alert, and many go with the royal party. The captain of the unicorn guard is alerted as they ride off. They ride with great speed to the Ruby Forest. They will meet the captain at Deer Meadow and notify him of the grave danger.

An hour has passed for the little prince. He makes his way through the secret doorway. Something catches his eye. There is a single purple flower growing at the doorway among all the vines. Prince Elgrin stops and picks it from its well-hidden spot. He will give it to his golden-haired friend for her birthday. He giggles and knows she will love it.

He must hurry now. Will he have enough time to see his new friend? He must.

Prince Elgrin squeezes through the small opening of the doorway and runs across the field to the spot where he first met the golden-haired Princess Arabella. He runs and runs but still does not see her. Then … there she is, sitting in the gardenia field.

Princess Arabella sits and picks gardenias. Pooks, Ellie, and Sirus are fluttering over the magnificent flowers. She giggles at the playfulness of her little friends. She looks up and sees Prince Elgrin. Very excited, she exclaims, "Look! Look! He's here! Prince Elgrin is here!"

She holds her flowers as she skips over to see Prince Elgrin in her beautiful sparkling dress and shoes. Her tiara sits on her long, curly, golden hair. She reaches the energy wall before Prince Elgrin and stands to wait.

Prince Elgrin sees her and his heart skips a beat. She is the most beautiful princess he has ever seen. He finally makes it to the energy wall. He knows that he does not have much time. He stops and catches his breath. "You came! Happy birthday, Princess Arabella!" he exclaims.

"Thank you, and happy birthday to you, Prince Elgrin. I am very glad you could come," says Princess Arabella.

"I didn't know if you would be able to come," says the prince.

"Sirus helped me to come and see you."

"Sirus helped me too!" says the amazed Prince Elgrin.

They explain how Sirus helped each of them. Giggling, they carry on their conversation.

CHAPTER 21

ing Gerald, Queen Amelia, and Prince Matthew, along
with the unicorn guards, continue to ride like the wind.
They have almost arrived at the gardenia field. They stop
and dismount. King Gerald helps Queen Amelia off her horse. They
walk into the gardenia field.

"There she is," Prince Matthew whispers. "Careful. Try not to
alert her just yet. We don't want to startle her into touching the wall.
But we must hurry—the sun is almost gone. Get down so we are not
spotted. Keep going." The royal family crouch down and make their
way to the edge of the gardenia field.

Meanwhile, back at Soomie Swamp, the Hagvillians are slowly
beginning to wake. Some of the guards try to awaken King Minos
and Queen Hag. After much shaking, a guard runs over to Soomie
Swamp with a bucket and fills it with water. He runs back to where
the king and queen lie. He lifts the bucket and empties it on King
Minos and Queen Hag. Gasping and spitting and shaking their royal
heads, they awaken to find themselves soaked.

"Wh-what has happened? Why did you douse us with water?"
yells King Minos.

"We've been potioned! Who would do such a thing? And put
the whole village to sleep!" screeches Queen Hag.

"We cannot find Prince Elgrin anywhere, your highness!" says one of the little green troll guards.

"Where is Hermie? The boys are always together! Find Hermie and we will find the prince!"

"Yes, your highness!" replies the troll. The guards help the royal couple to their feet.

The guards search frantically for the prince and his friend Hermie. "There!" One of the guards points to Hermie on the ground beside a little table. But Prince Elgrin is not there.

"Wake him!" yells another guard. Under a big splash of water, Hermie awakens sputtering and gasping. "Wh-what is going on?"

The guard helps Hermie to his feet and orders him to follow.

The king and queen await word from the guards. Queen Hag feels a tug on her royal cloak. There is a child at her side. "What is it?" harps the queen.

"I h-have seen P-Prince Elgrin," stammers the wee Hagvillian tot.

Queen Hag bends over and says, "You have seen Prince Elgrin? Where? Tell us, please!"

"W-well, I saw him by the Dreary Forest when I was coming from Soomie Swamp."

"Show me where?" asks King Minos.

The little Hagvillian points her dirty, bony finger to where she last saw the prince.

King Minos looks at Queen Hag. They know that they must hurry. They do not know how long they have been asleep.

"Here come the guards with Hermie," says the king. "Thank you, guards. Stand down."

The guards bow and back away a few feet, still standing near. The king kneels on one knee to speak with the young friend of Prince Elgrin.

"Hermie, where is Prince Elgrin? The prince could be in danger if we do not find him quickly," says King Minos.

"He has gone into the Dreary Forest with Sirus to see Princess Arabella," replies Hermie.

"Who in the world is Sirus?"

"Sirus is the little bluebird that we told you about. He sprinkled some magic dust on everyone so that Prince Elgrin could go and see Princess Arabella!"

"Thank you, Hermie. I must ask you to come with us so that you can show us where Prince Elgrin has gone," says the anxious king. "The guards will notify your mother and father of your whereabouts. We must go quickly; there is not much time before the moon rises."

King Minos and Queen Hag notify the guards to assemble and to get the boars and chariot ready. With Hermie, they set out for the royal barns. There they find the chariot and boars ready. Hermie gets in and seats himself on a cushion. Queen Hag steps in and seats herself on another cushion. King Minos jumps in and stands at the front of the chariot, grabbing the reins.

The king cracks the whip on the lead boars. With a great snort, the boars take off. The guards are close behind. Hermie points the way. They head into the Dreary Forest.

There is much decay, and the path narrows. The king stops and raises his hand. They must continue on foot. There are too many fallen trees along the path for the boars and chariot to cross. The guards dismount and tie their boars to some trees. King Minos, Queen Hag, and Hermie get out of the chariot and start the rather long walk through the forest to the secret door.

"Are we getting close?" exclaims the out-of-breath Queen Hag.

"There! There it is. Do you see it?" asks Hermie.

"See what?" retorts Queen Hag.

"The light in the forest. Do you see it?"

"I see it! Hurry, let's go!" yells King Minos.

They quicken their pace. There it is—the secret door, surrounded by moss and vines. It is barely recognizable in this huge forest except for the small beam of light that streams from behind it.

They near the door. The king motions for the guards to open it. Three guards push and heave until they hear a big *crack*. The door opens enough for them to go through.

They are all amazed at what they see: the green grass and immense energy wall. It goes on as far as the eye can see. They must hurry. In silence they walk through the field, looking for the prince before it is too late.

"There! There is Prince Elgrin beside the energy wall," says the little troll guard.

King Minos raises his hand and commands silence. They slowly make their way to the energy wall, where they see Prince Elgrin and Princess Arabella. The pair are talking and laughing, not noticing what is going on behind them.

Pook, Ellie, and Sirus do see what is happening and begin to flutter wildly.

"Don't bother me now. I am talking with my new friend. I will only be a minute. I must give my new friend his present." Princess Arabella giggles as she shoos her little friends away. "Look! I have picked you the most prized fragrant flowers of my kingdom!"

"I too have brought you something. It is also a flower, the only one of its kind. I have never seen anything like it. It grows on the secret door among the moss and vines. I have picked it for you," replies Prince Elgrin. "But how will I give it to you?"

"I don't know. Should we try to throw it through the energy wall? Maybe that will work!" says Princess Arabella.

"Do you think so?"

"Try it. If it doesn't, we will have at least seen each other's presents."

"Well, okay. Here it goes," says Prince Elgrin. He smells the flower. Then he pulls his arm back and flings the pretty little flower at the energy wall.

Poof! In a little cloud of smoke, the flower appears on the other side of the energy wall.

"It's here! It's here! You did it!" exclaims the princess. "Now I shall toss mine to you." Princess Arabella takes a breath, closes her eyes and tosses her flower at the energy wall. *Poof*! Through another little cloud of smoke, the gardenia lands at the feet of Prince Elgrin. The prince smiles.

The prince and princess gather their flowers and smile at each other. Suddenly they notice that their parents are standing at a distance behind them.

"Oh no! We are in trouble now! Quickly, touch my hand goodbye," asks Prince Elgrin. He looks at the princess, then at his parents, who stand only a few meters away now.

"Let's make a pact to be friends forever," the prince quickly says.

Their hands go up as if in slow motion, reaching toward the energy field. A thunderous "Noooooo!" is bellowed out by both sides. Horrified looks are on the royal families' faces when the children's hands go up. The families lunge for their children. Will they reach them in time?

Princess Arabella and Prince Elgrin turn to see what all the yelling is about. They see their families' faces curled in horror. Then they turn back to each other. Their hands are only a few inches apart when—

PART TWO

CHAPTER 22

Princess Arabella turns her head as if in slow motion toward Prince Elgrin. Her arm is outstretched, just wanting to touch the prince's hand.

Suddenly she seems to be pulled backward at an alarming speed, dragged far away from her prince. So much is happening around her. The princess slumps over and faints.

Princess Arabella hangs limply in Prince Matthew's arms as he jumps onto his horse. Gently holding his little sister, he swiftly rides back to the palace, leaving the guards and King Gerald to deal with the energy wall until he gets back. Queen Amelia follows the prince on her steed, wanting to be there when Princess Arabella awakes from her fainting spell. Prince Elgrin watches in horror as Princess Arabella is whisked off to her kingdom, Crystal City.

At that very moment, Prince Elgrin feels an intense pain. It is as though his arm is being jerked from the socket. He turns and sees his mother, Queen Hag, at the other end of his painful arm. She pulls her son close and, sobbing, hugs him. Prince Elgrin slowly tucks his flower into his pocket as his mother squeezes him ever so tightly. The queen takes him by the hand. They walk to the big door at the edge of the woods in silence.

Prince Elgrin knows if he utters a single word, he will be in even bigger trouble than he already is. The only thought in the prince's head is the beautiful Princess Arabella. How close he came to touching her hand! Oh, how he wishes he could have stayed a while longer and talked with her. *One day, I will*, he thought. *One day.*

CHAPTER 23

Queen Hag and Prince Elgrin make their way to the huge wooden door at the edge of the forest, the only way back to Hagville. As Prince Elgrin follows his mother through the door, he glances into the vines to see if he can see another flower—a flower just like the one he gave to Princess Arabella. There is none. That means the flower is as beautiful and as rare as his new friend. Smiling, Prince Elgrin is happy as he gently pats his pocket where his flower is. The royal pair trudges on through the Dreary Forest. It is a long journey over dead trees, twigs, shrubs, and thistles.

Queen Hag is rather winded by now and is looking for a lovely spot to rest her weary bones. She stops at a very large dead tree and sits down. Prince Elgrin sits beside his mother. A few minutes pass. Queen Hag finally speaks. "What in the world were you thinking?"

"Well, Mother, it was my friend's birthday today, too, so I just wanted to wish her a happy birthday!" says Prince Elgrin.

"You should know how dangerous it is to be in the Dreary Forest alone! What if something had happened to you? How would we have known where you were? And what about that fairy potion you used to put us all to sleep?" bellowed Queen Hag.

"Mother! Stop! I am very sorry! I did not mean to worry you and Father. I was on the most amazing adventure. I d-did not think it was d-dangerous," stammers a sobbing Prince Elgrin.

"Well, that's right, son. You didn't think. So that is why your father and I have decided that you will be going to military school, since you tell me you are interested in adventure. Military school should give you all the adventure you need!" lectures the angry queen.

"There! There it is! The chariot." Prince Elgrin runs to the chariot. He can't wait to get back to the castle in Hagville. He has had a wonderful day. Maybe Hermie will be back soon also.

Queen Hag stomps over to the chariot. Prince Elgrin is already sitting on his rumpled little seat with his head down. His mother hoists her hefty frame into the chariot. She stands as she cracks the whip on the lead boar's snout. With heavy squeals, the boars break into a good run through the Dreary Forest. Up and down the little prince bounces on his seat. Thinking that this is rather fun, he lets out a wee laugh. To his dismay, his mother shoots him a nasty look. He keeps quiet the rest of the way to Hagville.

They finally arrive at the gates of Hagville. The whip cracks again over the boars' heads. They maneuver through the humongous timber gates at the entrance and carry on until they reach the castle tram. The royal pair gets out of the chariot, and the boar masters take the boars and the chariot to the stables. Queen Hag and Prince Elgrin walk quickly to the tram.

Screeeeeeech! Claaaaaaaank! Squeal! goes the tram as it is slowly lowered from the walkway high above. Queen Hag and Prince Elgrin are greeted by one of the queen's troll guards, who let the two into the tram. They are about to be hoisted up when the prince sees his little friend Hermie heading to the tram, walking ever so slowly.

With a huge bump, the tram comes to a stop at the top of the walkway. The little green troll lets Queen Hag and Prince Elgrin out. Prince Elgrin dashes out of the tram and runs to the castle with the queen in close pursuit, They reach the huge wooden doors of the castle, and the queen reaches over and pulls the door knocker and lets it go. A thunderous boom is heard outside the castle, and the doors open. The little troll guards greet the royals as they enter.

The queen and prince carry on into the kitchen to see if a snack can be made for the hungry prince. He heads over to the huge wooden table, pulls out a chair, and sits down. He reaches toward a bowl filled with pastries and grabs one.

"Prince Elgrin, I want you to go to your room this instant!" orders the queen. "I need to speak to your father to decide what we are to do to remove temptation of that girl."

"That girl has a name. She is Princess Arabella! And she is my friend, and there is nothing you can do about it!" sobs the prince.

"Well! We will certainly see about that! Now, to your room!" shrieks the angry queen.

"Good night!" The prince goes upstairs.

Prince Elgrin stomps his feet as he walks slowly. He doesn't know what to do. He keeps walking through the great room to the foyer and the stairs.

Looking through a door under the stairs are the two little rats, chattering about what has just happened. The rats are worried. Vulture has made sure that every creature in Hagville is on alert until the moon shines full tonight. The prince is home now, so Hagville is safe. The two nosy little rats scamper back into their hovel and slam the door as they usually do.

Prince Elgrin lets out a little laugh. He slowly climbs the long staircase up to the second floor, then makes his way down the long hallway to his room. He opens his door, turns, and shuts it. He takes off his royal birthday clothes and carefully removes the gardenia from his pocket. He walks to his closet and rummages through it. The prince is on a mission.

"Ah! Here it is," exclaims the prince. Out of the closet he pulls what looks like a short tree trunk. He goes to the bed and sits down. He holds the bottom of this special box with one hand and twists the top with the other. It opens. Prince Elgrin gently puts the gardenia into his special box and slides the lid closed. He gets up and puts his special box on the mantel above his fireplace.

Prince Elgrin puts on his pajamas, slides into his rumpled royal bed, and snuggles in for the night.

CHAPTER 24

Prince Matthew rides hard and fast. He finally arrives at the palace with his sister still slumped over his arm. He slowly dismounts from his horse. Prince Matthew adjusts the princess and gently carries her up the stairs to the palace doors. Servants come running in as the prince enters the main area of the palace. Prince Matthew hands the sleeping princess over to one of the servants, nods, then heads back out of the palace.

Prince Matthew runs over to the stables for the fresh horse. The prince hears the clatter of hooves and glances over his shoulder to see his mother ride in. He hurries back to the palace to help her dismount.

Queen Amelia hugs her son and says, "Oh Matthew, that was far too close. Hopefully there will never be a next time, but as we both know, there will be. But she will be older then!"

"What do you mean, next time?" asks Prince Matthew.

"Pay me no mind, my son. Those are just the upset words of a worried mother," says the queen.

"If you are sure that you and Arabella are going to be all right, I will go," declares the prince.

"Thank you, son. We will be fine. We have many servants to take care of us until you return with your father. Safe journey!" Queen Amelia calls as she watches her son run off. With a great sigh of relief, the queen walks up the stairs to the palace to check on her daughter.

She enters the large crystal doors into the main room. Servants come running to her and let her know that the young princess is all tucked in and sleeping in her bed. Queen Amelia thanks the servants and goes up the stairs to the princess's bedroom. She slides the door open. Looking inside, she sees her daughter sound asleep like a little angel, snuggled up with a teddy bear.

The queen enters her daughter's room and shuts the door. Queen Amelia sits down beside the sleeping princess. She strokes her daughter's forehead. Princess Arabella stirs and stretches and opens her eyes.

"Mumsy? What are you doing here?" asks the sleepy little princess. "And who is Prince Elgrin?"

"Prince Elgrin? Well. He … I don't know any Prince Elgrin, my dear. You must have been dreaming," says the worried queen.

"Dreaming? Are you sure? It seemed so real. The energy wall and the flower, just a dream?"

"I am sorry, my dear, but, yes, it was just a dream. Lay your head back down and go to sleep. You are going to have a grand day with all your friends."

The angelic princess does as her mother tells her and is sound asleep in minutes. The queen stays for a while and then heads for the main room to see if there is news of King Gerald and Prince Matthew's return.

A knock is heard at the huge crystal doors. A guard answers. Before him stands Galena with Zues on her arm. She carries a small satchel. Galena pulls off the hood of her long cloak, bows to the guards, and enters the palace. "I must speak with Queen Amelia. It is of the utmost urgency!" exclaims the royal seer.

A guard assists Galena to the planning room to wait for Queen Amelia.

Queen Amelia is informed of her guest's arrival and promptly goes to the planning room to see why Galena has come. The queens worries. Galena would come to the palace only if it is a dire emergency. The distraught queen enters the planning room to find Galena sitting at her little table by the royal thrones—the very spot where she sat only days before. Queen Amelia smiles. "Good evening, Galena."

"Good evening, your highness. I apologize for the late hour, but it is not over, my queen. Because Princess Arabella did not succeed in making contact with Prince Elgrin through the energy wall, she will be troubled every year upon her birthday. The pull upon her will be great to see the prince, but we can stop it," says Galena.

"But how, Galena? How can we stop the prophecy?"

"There is but one way. If we can stop her from remembering meeting Prince Elgrin, we may be able to hold off the prophecy."

"Are you sure it will work?"

"I have brought a potion with me. It is the only way to make the princess forget. If the prince has touched her heart, then it is too late. She will forever pine for what she knows is to be. The princess is young. With enough potion, she will not remember, and our world can be saved."

"Galena, we must try! We must do all that we can to save our world! We cannot risk any breach of the energy wall."

"Yes, my queen, I understand. Are you ready to administer the potion to your sleeping princess before she asks too many questions about this evening's events?"

"Yes. If you are ready, we will go up and see Princess Arabella." Queen Amelia motions for Galena to follow her.

Galena gathers a few things from the table, says a few words, and puts her things in her satchel. She is now ready, and so is the potion she has made for the princess.

Galena follows Queen Amelia through the palace to the princess's room. Once inside, Queen Amelia makes sure that Princess Arabella is still fast asleep. She motions for Galena to come over to the bed. Galena glides over, opens her satchel, and pulls out a little vial. She opens the vial and bends over the sleeping Princess Arabella. Galena pours three drops of thick, sparkling liquid onto the forehead of the princess. The potion is quickly absorbed. Galena once again goes into her satchel and pulls out a small crystal wand. On the end of the wand is a glowing emerald. Galena waves the wand over the princess's forehead three times while chanting a verse in a language that only she knows.

"There, it is done," says Galena. "The princess will have no memory of the events of this evening, Queen Amelia."

Queen Amelia leans over her sleeping daughter as Galena puts the crystal wand in her satchel. She can hear Zues call. It is time to go. Galena's work for the moment is done. She bows graciously to Queen Amelia.

"Thank you, Galena. The servants will see you out. I shall stay with my daughter for a while longer," says Queen Amelia. She hugs Galena.

Galena is escorted from the room. She waits as the guards open the huge crystal doors for her and Zues, and they leave.

"Well, Zues, my trusted friend, all will be well at the palace for a time now. We can rest and gather our powers. The next time it happens, I do not know if anyone will have the power to stop the prophecy," Galena whispers as they walk back to their home on Mystic Mountain.

The queen hears a commotion coming from the main area downstairs. She quietly gets up, leaving the princess sleeping, and proceeds downstairs. She hears King Gerald and Prince Matthew. They have come home. Hoping that all is well at the energy wall, she rushes into the arms of her husband. "Is everything all right, my dear?" she asks.

"Yes, all has been secured. There has been no breach. It is clear on both sides of the wall. We will be safe for some years now. We must be wary and ever vigilant to guard the wall so this never happens again—although I know one day it will," replies King Gerald.

The royals are exhausted and ready for sleep. Queen Amelia tells King Gerald and Prince Matthew of Galena's visit and the measures that have been taken to protect Princess Arabella. They are all in agreement and are very relieved by this turn of events.

The royal couple say good night to their son and go up to bed. There will be much to do tomorrow. There will be a day or two of cleanup after the big party. But for now, everyone must rest. Sleep overtakes King Gerald and Queen Amelia quickly.

CHAPTER 25

In the meantime, back in Hagville, the angry Queen Hag is pacing back and forth in the foyer, waiting for King Minos to come back from the energy wall. The two little rats are also pacing and wondering what is going on. The nosy pair is just waiting for the chance to spread a bit of juicy gossip to all their animal friends.

The squeal of the tram can be heard in the distance, and Queen Hag hurries over to the large wooden doors. The doors spring open, and there stands King Minos and his trusted advisor, Draco. The king puts Draco down, and he scurries on his long, furry, spider legs to see the rats. After much chatter, the rats run back to their hovel under the stairs and slam the door.

King Minos looks and feels exhausted. Queen Hag hugs her king. He informs her of the events that occurred after she took Prince Elgrin back to Hagville. There was no contact from either side. The children were swiftly taken out of the situation. The huge wooden door in the Dreary Forest has been secured, and the trail has been modified. No one will find the door to the energy wall ever again.

The king is quite pleased. Queen Hag, however, is another story. In fact, she is quite upset while she talks with King Minos. The pair decides to sleep and ponder what to do next about Prince Elgrin's troubles.

King Minos tells Queen Hag that the Ebbeney Oracle was sent for. The Ebbeney Oracle will arrive by morning, and they will talk about events and deal with Prince Elgrin. The exhausted pair head upstairs to crawl into bed and rest until morning.

—⟋ɯ⟍—

Morning arrives in Hagville. Queen Hag hears a familiar caw outside. It is Sparaxis, which means that the Ebbeney Oracle is nearby. *At last we can save Prince Elgrin*, thinks Queen Hag.

A thunderous boom comes from the palace door. Queen Hag hurries down the stairs to the main area.

King Minos and Queen Hag greet the Ebbeney Oracle. The three walk to the planning room. They take their seats at the table in the corner. The Ebbeney Oracle reaches into her satchel and takes out a black cloth out. She lays it on the table. She then takes all her little stones and bones and throws them in a jumble on the black cloth. The Ebbeney Oracle performs the same ritual three times, mumbling, as the king and queen watch. Then she is done. She gathers all her things from the table and sets them back into her satchel. Now she can speak with the king and queen about their troubles.

"What is it, Ebbeney?" asks the queen.

"I have the memory-dimmer potion you asked for, King Minos," says the Ebbeney Oracle.

"Thank you, great oracle. But what news do you have of the prophecy?" asks King Minos.

"You are very lucky for now, your highnesses. But the prophecy is not over yet. There will be a time of several years during which you will not hear mention or see sign of the prophecy. Then there will be one more moon—a moon blue and cold, just like the moon that rose on the eve of the prince's birth. It will rise once again. Only this time, it will grow dark with an eclipse. It will be the most powerful of all. It will be the final moon of the prophecy. That will be the telling of our kingdoms. The signs will begin at the start of the new year, and we will have to prepare for what the signs say. It is not time right now for worrying about the moon. We must help the prince to forget what has happened. Shall we go and see him now?"

King Minos leads the way. Queen Hag and the Ebbeney Oracle follow closely behind. King Minos opens the door to his son's room. There is the prince, still fast asleep in his rumpled bed. The Ebbeney Oracle walks in first as the king holds the door open. She reaches the bed and takes her satchel from her side. The oracle pulls out a small vial with the memory potion in it. The Ebbeney Oracle has instructed the king and queen on the procedure for using the potion correctly in order for it to erase the prince's memory. This potion can be used on a subject only one time; it is too dangerous to ever try it again. King Minos and Queen Hag anxiously watch the oracle apply the potion to the sleeping Prince Elgrin.

First, the Ebbeney Oracle opens the vial and passes it under the nose of the sleeping prince three times. Then she puts three drops on the top of the prince's head and rubs his head in a counterclockwise motion three times. Now she is ready for the last and most important step: three drops on his tongue. She is careful not to let any roll off, for to lose any would lessen the strength of the potion.

She drops the first bead on the prince's tongue. Drop number two also hits its target. But just as the oracle squeezes out drop number three, a vulture screeches outside, startling the oracle. Her arm moves ever so slightly. The drop of potion slowly falls down, and hits Prince Elgrin's tongue. Some rolls off, foaming, and *poof,* it is gone.

The Ebbeney Oracle hopes enough of the third drop was on target to dim the prince's memory for long enough. The oracle turns to the king and queen and nods her head. She stands, gathers her things, and leaves the castle.

The king and queen gaze down at their sleeping child. The queen comments, "Look at our prince. He sleeps so soundly. He will have no recollection of the events that have transpired over the last few days."

"I am glad for that, my dear. We must keep a keen eye on our prince these next years. As he comes of age, sending him off to military academy is the right thing. The military academy will give him all the right traits to make him a great leader. Maybe he will forget the princess and find a more suitable bride. If he chooses a bride from his world, then we will not have to worry. The prophecy will no longer be a factor," states King Minos.

As the worried king and queen carry on conversing about the situation, they hear a faint sound. The royal couple turn to see their son stirring and stretching, waking from his seemingly uninterrupted sleep.

Opening his eyes, Prince Elgrin looks rather startled to find his parents standing over his bed, smiling. "Wh-what is going on? Why are you both here? Am I in trouble?" asks the perplexed prince.

"Slow down. You are not in trouble. Your father and I came in to wake you this morning for breakfast, that is all. Now hurry and get ready. I am sure that Cook has prepared many of your favorites today," says Queen Hag.

"Yes, Mother. I will hurry and get ready. I will meet you and Father downstairs in the kitchen." Prince Elgrin smiles.

King Minos and Queen Hag leave their son's room and head for the kitchen. The walk downstairs is somber. All is quiet in the castle this morning. Even the rats are not scurrying around gossiping. Everyone is quiet after the events of the previous day.

The prince hurries and dons his clothes for the day. Feeling a bit strange, he sits on his bed. He thinks of the grand birthday celebration the day before and smiles. But wait—he doesn't remember coming home. The last thing he remembers is having a wonderful meal and planning something with his friend Hermie. But what was it? He tries, but he just can't remember. He decides he will have to ask his parents at breakfast.

Prince Elgrin bolts from his room and runs down the hall to the stairs. He lies on the railing and slides down, hopeful that he will not be caught. *Swoooooosh*! *Bump*! The prince slams into the finial at the end of the rail. He jumps off and runs into the kitchen.

His parents are seated at the large wooden table, already eating their breakfast. The prince smiles and sits down on a huge chair across from them. Prince Elgrin begins to eat his breakfast. "Mother, what happened last night? I am trying to remember, but I just can't. The last thing I remember is planning something with Hermie, and the rest is blank. Do you remember?"

"Why, yes, dear. You and Hermie were so busy playing and planning that you fell asleep at the table during your celebration. Some of the servants had to carry you home, and we put you to bed. You must have been exhausted after all the celebrating you and Hermie were doing, running and laughing and playing with all your friends."

"Can I go out and play with Hermie?"

"Not today, son. Everyone is involved in the cleanup of yesterday's celebration, and there is too much to do. You should have a quiet day inside and not get in the way," replies his mother.

"Well, can I help? You know that I am a good helper, Mother," boasts the prince.

"I suppose you can help. Be mindful of the elders, please. And listen to your guard. He will let you know what you can do," says King Minos.

"Guard? What guard? Why do I need a guard, Father?"

"You and your friend Hermie have been getting into too much trouble lately. That is why you will listen to your personal guard or else stay in the castle. The choice is yours."

"All right. You win. I will help on the grounds with Hermie and my guard," sighs the disgruntled prince.

Prince Elgrin leaves the kitchen. He scampers out of the castle to the tram. The little green troll guard lets the prince onto the tram, and with the usual *bump*, *grind*, and *screeeeech*, the prince arrives on the ground. The green troll guard opens the door. The prince runs out and, with a quick wave, he is gone.

CHAPTER 26

Prince Elgrin runs as fast as his legs can carry him. He soon reaches Soomie Swamp. The servants are gathering up dishes and things from the celebration the night before. The guards stand at attention and scan the area for intruders, while paying attention every moment to the whereabouts of the prince.

The prince also keeps scanning the area, hoping to spot Hermie. He walks around, looking for his friend and asking almost everyone who is cleaning up. Not having any luck, the prince decides to go back to the castle and check on his friend later at Hermie's hovel.

Prince Elgrin forlornly strolls back to the castle.

At Hermie's hovel, the only ones left at the breakfast table are Hermie, his mother Edwina, and his father Trolby. All is unusually quiet this morning. Hermie's parents don't look too happy. The celebration turned into a disaster, what with the children escaping to the Dreary Forest and an angry Queen Hag. What will happen? No one knows, but one thing is for sure. Hermie must not mention a word about what happened to Prince Elgrin during the celebration, or they will be banished from Hagville, the only home they have ever known.

"Father, may I go out to Soomie Swamp and help Saggerella with the cleanup?" asks Hermie.

"I am sorry, son, but today you must stay inside. The events of yesterday are very worrisome. You have been forbidden to see Prince Elgrin for a period of seven days. After the seven days, you may see your friend if you pay close attention to the guard. That is all, Hermie. Now go and play in your room. I am sure that Vincent would like to play with you," says his father.

"B-but, Father, seven days! I cannot see my friend for seven days?" asks Hermie.

"Yes, seven days. And you must swear, as the whole of Hagville has, that you will never speak of Princess Arabella ever again. You must never mention her name in front of Prince Elgrin. Is that understood?" asks Trolby.

"Yes, but why?"

"It is a very dangerous time, my son, a very dangerous time. The prince would be in grave danger if you caused him to remember the princess. That is all that I can tell you for the moment. When you are older, we will discuss more. And speaking of becoming older, we will be enrolling you in the military academy soon. You will be of age to begin attending. It will likely keep you out of trouble!" Trolby says. He smiles from just the corner of his mouth.

"Yes, sir," replies a greatly saddened Hermie. *Seven days I have to stay away from Prince Elgrin! Seven days! And military academy! What am I going to do? I need to speak with my friend. I need to see him now!* thinks Hermie.

Upset, he gets off his chair and pushes it under the slab table. Leaving his father and mother still talking, Hermie goes back to his room. He knows what he has to do.

In his room, Hermie shuts and locks the door. He goes over to his rumpled bed, hops on it, and crawls to his window. He sticks his head out and looks around. *Not a Hagvillian is in sight.*

Hermie jumps out the window and runs to the shed in the back. There he takes a crumpled piece of parchment from his pocket, along with charcoal to scribe with, and begins to write.

Prince Elgrin—

Mother and Father just told me that I am not allowed to see you for seven days. I will try to find out what is going on. We will meet in three nights, just after the moon rises, at the boar barns. I will sneak away, making sure not to be seen.

H.

Hermie rolls the parchment up and ties it onto Vincent. Hermie gives Vincent instructions and watches him run out of the shed.

Vincent knows the route like the back of his little paw. Dodging and darting through Hagville, hoping not to be spotted by the vultures, he scampers ever so close to the castle There is a great commotion outside the huge doors, and Vincent cannot gain access without being seen. The little rat knows exactly what to do. His rat cousins live inside with Queen Hag and King Minos. All he has to do is give their special whistle, and his cousins will come running through their tunnel inside the castle.

Vincent takes in a deep breath, again being ever so careful not to be seen. He puckers his little rat lips and whistles, a sound so high-pitched that no one else can hear.

Vincent sits and waits. He waits and listens. He hears it: a faint rustling of dead leaves. He sits very still. Ah! There they are. Vincent's cousins run to him. The three rats keep within the shelter of a holly berry bush. They chatter so quietly and quickly that no one hears.

Before long, the rats scatter. The cousins scamper back to the tunnel with the note Hermie wrote. Vincent scurries for home.

Prince Elgrin sits in his room, trying to concentrate on the book he is reading. He hears a little rap on the rat door. (On the side of the fireplace is a secret door to the rat tunnels.) Prince Elgrin jumps off the bed and goes to the fireplace. Out pops Omar, one of the resident rats.

"Hello, Omar! What is going on down there?" giggles the prince.

"Squeak! Squeak!" says Omar. He shows the prince the rolled-up scroll, which he holds with his tail. Prince Elgrin bends over and picks up the scroll.

On top of the mantle is a bowl. The prince reaches into it and grabs a peanut. He hands it to Omar, who immediately snatches it and gobbles it up. Omar squeaks and runs back through the little rat door. The only evidence that he was there is a pile of peanut shells. The prince turns back to the scroll, laughing, and reads it.

Okay, time to find out what is happening here at the castle. Things have been a little strange since I woke up, thinks the prince. He decides to snoop around to see if he can find out what is going on.

CHAPTER 27

Morning comes quickly in Crystal City. The palace bustles with servants scurrying here and there, cleaning up from the previous night's celebration. The grounds are a hub of activity. There are wagons lined up for a mile, waiting to wheel in and pick up the tables, chairs, barbecues, and other remains.

Inside the palace, the royal family is still seated at the breakfast table, talking and laughing about the night before. They are ever so careful not to mention the incident at the energy wall.

"Do you have any special plans with your friends today? Maybe watch all the movers clean the grounds? I know how you like to do that," says the queen.

"Oh yes, Mumsy. Pooks and Ellie are in the gardens waiting for me right now. I have to hurry," says the excited princess.

"All right. Be good then. Have fun!" yell her parents as the princess skips out of the room.

"Arabella has no recollection of events after supper last night," says the king.

"Thank goodness for Galena. Arabella can be safe for a long time if she does not regain her memory," says Queen Amelia.

"Yes, it lightens my heart knowing we have many years before we need worry about Arabella and the prince," replies King Gerald.

"I must go to the stables now, or I will be late for a meeting with the unicorn guards. I need an update on the status of the energy wall," Prince Matthew says.

"Goodbye, son. Have a good day," says his mother.

"Bye, Mother. Goodbye, Father," says Prince Matthew. He turns and leaves the table. He heads to the stables, where he is meeting the unicorn guards.

King Gerald leans over and kisses his wife. He rises and walks to the planning room. The king also has much work to do after the celebration.

Queen Amelia rises, leaves the kitchen, and goes into the sitting room. The beautiful queen loves to tend her orchids and play the organ in the sitting room. The sitting room has walls with windows all around, in a circular shape, to let as much light in as possible for the exotic flowers.

In the lush flower gardens, the princess and all her friends play. Pooks and Ellie flutter around, playing tag with the princess. Chipper, the palace squirrel, chases a huge walnut down a hill and into the flower beds. The two wood sprites giggle and point. Chipper finally jumps on the nut as it rolls, only to lose his footing. He and his nut roll over and over and over.

Chipper finally stops rolling and comes to a stop with a thud against a big tree trunk in the middle of the flower garden. He is lying down, shaking his little head, while the wood sprites are rolling on the ground laughing. Princess Arabella holds her belly, laughing also. It is such a funny sight. Angry little Chipper grabs his nut and hustles back up the hill to his nest in an old fir tree.

The trio run over to a blanket on the grass and lie down to catch their breaths. Princess Arabella gazes into the sky. The shape of the clouds seem to remind her of something. She just cannot remember what. The princess smiles, trying to remember.

Soon there is a buzzing and fluttering around her head. Princess Arabella slowly turns her head and notices Pooks flipping back and forth, showing off to Ellie. Once again the trio rolls over laughing.

It is time for the little princess to head home. The wood sprites fly to the huge flower gardens, and the princess skips back to the palace.

CHAPTER 28

Back in Hagville, Prince Elgrin is on a mission. The prince must find out what he can about what is going on at the castle. Everyone is secretive and whispers all the time. The young prince and his friend need to know what is happening around them.

With that thought, Prince Elgrin opens the door of his room and peeks out to see if anything is going on in the hallway. There are no servants or guards or helpers of any kind. *Where am I going to find out any information? The rats! I can speak with the rats, Omar and Dee. I am sure they will tell me something They know all the happenings at the castle,* thinks Prince Elgrin.

He sneaks along the hall and down the huge wooden staircase, paying close attention to the whereabouts of everyone so he can arrange some privacy with Omar and Dee. The prince strolls around the staircase, making it look like he is going to a closet. He quickly looks around. "The coast is clear," he mumbles to himself and squats by the little rat door at the bottom of the staircase. Prince Elgrin knocks ever so quietly on the rat door.

He hears chatter before Omar opens the door and peeks outside. Omar sees Prince Elgrin and opens the door wider. Omar lets out a little chatter, and Dee quickly comes running over. The rats chatter for a moment more, then wait for the prince to speak.

"Omar! Dee! Nice to see you. I am sure you know that something strange is going on here at the castle. Have you two heard anything or seen anything?' asks the prince.

"Squeak, squeak. Why, no, Prince Elgrin. The only news at the castle is that you are going to attend military academy, just like your father King Minos did when he was young. But that is all we have heard happening, sir," says suspicious Omar.

Omar looks at Dee. Dee looks back at Omar. She just shakes her little nose back and forth, confirming that no new information is being kept from the prince. Prince Elgrin thanks the pair, and they scurry off behind the rat door and slam it.

The prince is perplexed at the course of events since his party. *Maybe there really is no mystery, and I am just being sent off to the military academy. Oh well, it is not so bad then. Maybe some of my friends will be going also,* thinks the little prince.

The days slowly pass. Now the prince can go and find his friend Hermie. Bolting out of the castle—with his parents' permission—Prince Elgrin runs to the tram and waits to go down to the ground. At last the tram arrives. The green troll guard opens the door for the prince, and the tram is sent down to the ground. Prince Elgrin thanks the troll and steps out. He looks toward Soomie Swamp to see if he can spot his friend.

Prince Elgrin does not see Hermie. He keeps walking, knowing with every step that he is being closely watched by a guard. The prince wonders if Hermie has been able to sneak out of his hovel.

Prince Elgrin stops and scans the area. Over by the swamp, he thinks he sees his friend. Yes! Hermie is sitting and playing in the sand on the beach. Prince Elgrin walks over and sits beside his friend. Hermie looks up and smiles his little troll smile. The prince smiles back.

"Hermie, did you find anything out?" asks the prince.

"Nah, not a thing. Sorry. Everyone is talking about you and the military academy," says Hermie. "And guess what? My parents are sending me there too. I am not very happy, but I guess I have to go.

The only good thing is that you and I will both be going to the same school. That will be a lot of fun, don't you think?"

"Military academy? Whoa! I didn't think the big mystery would be about me going to the military academy. I guess we are almost of age, and we must attend," says the worried prince.

CHAPTER 29

Many years slowly pass.

Prince Elgrin goes about his daily routine: passing the time with his friend, attending the military academy, and having fun at Soomie Swamp. But in the Ruby Forest, it is quite another story. There is a new presence there, and Prince Matthew and his forces are sent out to see what it is.

The troop rides fast and hard to get to the south end of the forest. It seems there may be a breach from the Kingdom of Likeria. It also appears that there is a weakness in the energy wall.

Remember, it is the ninth year of the treaty. The wall may be opening for free travel. If that is the case, we must post a sentry to seek identification of all who pass, thinks Prince Matthew.

They are almost there, and Prince Matthew can see something. In the distance are several riders on horseback. Strangely, they seem to be sparring with someone on a white horse. The rider on the white horse is covered completely in a white uniform, including a white mask and cape. The closer Prince Matthew and his troops get, the louder the sounds become. The sounds are … laughter!

The group is sparring with long poles, trying to knock each other off their horses. The bunch is startled by Prince Matthew's approach. A rider is knocked off his horse. The other riders grab his arm and hoist him back onto his horse. He grabs the reins and the whole party gallops off. But before they flee through the energy wall, Prince Matthew catches a glimpse of a strange mark on the hip of the white horse. The mark is circular with an eagle in the center of it. Prince Matthew has never seen such a mark before. He decides to ask his father, King Gerald, if he has knowledge of such a mark.

Prince Matthew and his troops ride along the energy wall to see if they can find out how the intruders entered the Ruby Forest.

"The wall is definitely weakening. We will keep a detail at the entrance. When the wall does dematerialize, we will have some control as to who may enter our world," commands Prince Matthew.

"Yes, sir," replies the unicorn guard.

Prince Matthew turns his steed and gallops back to the palace. He strides into the sitting room, looking for his father. Sitting on a huge, padded armchair is the king.

"Father!" yells Prince Matthew.

"Yes! I am here!"

"Have you ever seen this mark?" the prince asks, showing his father a drawing of the mark on the white horse's hip. The king has a look of shock on his worn face.

King Gerald stands and paces back and forth. Prince Matthew is quite confused. "Father, what is it? You know what this mark means, don't you?" asks the perplexed prince.

"Yes, but only because I saw an old drawing many years ago. It is the sign of the ancient protectors. They are known as the Likerians, the keepers of the kingdoms. They were trained to protect all of our worlds.

"It does not matter now, son. We shall throw a welcoming ball for them when the doorway opens in the energy wall," explains King Gerald. "The energy wall is slowly dematerializing. Invitations must be sent to the kingdom in the new world. The grand ball will commence in three days, and we must prepare."

The days pass and the day of the ball arrives. Crystal Palace is all hustle and bustle again. Staff flit around with tablecloths, flower arrangements, and food. Everyone dresses in their royal finery.

Princess Arabella is dressed by her handmaids. She looks quite beautiful in a yellow ball gown, complete with tiara and shoes. Princess Arabella twirls in front of her full-length mirror to admire herself. She sees her mother enter the room. "Mother, how do I look?" asks the princess.

"Oh, my dear, you are absolutely beautiful! You are growing into a wonderful young woman. Your father and I are so proud of you," Queen Amelia says, with a tear rolling down her cheek.

"Thank you," the princess says with a smile. "Maybe my brother will find a bride tonight. I am tired of waiting, ha-ha."

"You may be right, my dear. It surely is time he takes a bride. It would be lovely if he did before you were to go off to school," replies Queen Amelia. "Listen, the horn is sounding. We must hurry. The dignitary parade will begin soon."

"Yes, Mother. I am ready. Let's go!"

The royal pair leaves the room and goes to meet King Gerald and Prince Matthew outside the royal ballroom. The guards open the doors and announce the royal family. The dignitary procession begins. The royal family stands to greet these distinguished guests at the end of a long red carpet that runs the whole length of the center of the ballroom.

With all the guests in place, the festivities begin. All the available maidens slowly gather by Prince Matthew. The dancing starts, and laughter and merriment ensue among all the guests.

A horn sounds. The dancing stops. Everyone looks toward the sound.

The double doors swing open, and there stands the most beautiful maiden Prince Matthew has ever seen. She has flowing blonde hair and piercing blue eyes that could stop a man in his tracks. Prince Matthew cannot take his gaze from hers. He is drawn to this woman. He leaves the dozen maidens at his side and slowly walks to the newcomer.

"Princess Likeria from the Kingdom of Likeria," a guard announces.

Her parents and other royal guests from the Kingdom of Likeria follow the princess inside. Prince Matthew bows and holds his hand out to the princess. She graciously places her hand into his. It's like magic. The pair begin to dance. The music plays slowly. They glide as one on the dance floor.

Prince Matthew looks adoringly at his princess. He now knows who his bride will be. Princess Likeria is his chosen one. The prince and princess never leave each other's arms on the dance floor.

The king and queen of Likeria summon their daughter when it is time to leave. Business has been done. The princess turns her head and bows to Prince Matthew and the Crystal Palace royals.

Prince Matthew is aghast at what he sees—the same symbol that was on the white horse of the mystery rider at the south end of the wall!

Was the rider her? Prince Matthew must find out. Princess Likeria is a member of the Ancient Protectors.

Prince Matthew will announce his decision to his parents in the morning. What a wonderful night for the royal family. What a wonderful night indeed.

As he has planned, Prince Matthew announces to his parents that he has chosen his bride. Word will be sent to the Kingdom of Likeria, and they will wait for a reply.

Without delay, a reply is received from the Kingdom of Likeria. The royal wedding will take place in one month. Let the royal courtship begin. Prince Matthew packs his things to go to the Kingdom of Likeria and court his beautiful bride-to-be.

"We won't be seeing your brother for several weeks now, Arabella," says King Gerald.

"Why, Father? What has happened?"

"Well, at the ball your brother chose a bride. Princess Likeria has agreed. Prince Matthew is going to the Kingdom of Likeria to court his chosen one. The wedding will be in one month."

"I am so happy, Father! I cannot wait for the wedding!" says the happy Princess Arabella.

"Yes, the whole kingdom is very happy for our prince. That is not all the good news we have to share. You, my darling daughter, will be going to the Academy of Etiquette and Epicure soon. It will also be a wonderful time for you. You will leave after the wedding," says King Gerald.

Princess Arabella looks shocked. "How soon after the wedding?"

"I am sorry to say you have only seven days before you leave. And one more thing, my dear—you will have guards with you at all times. There will be two of them, and you must follow their direction. You need to be protected."

"Two guards, Father?"

"Yes, two guards."

"All right, Father."

The angry princess turns and stomps out of the room. She decides to go for a walk in the gardens, the place that makes her feel safe and makes her smile with all the memories of the silly games she used to play with her friends. The forlorn princess takes in a deep breath and suddenly remembers: a memory of the smell of the gardenias and a strange-looking boy. She startles herself. *Hmmmmm, who was that boy? I don't remember having a playmate, let alone a little boy. I have my dog Monty and all the little wood sprites. I will have to think about that. I also wonder who the guards will be. I hope it's not the horrible two who went to the ball with me*, thinks the princess.

The weeks pass quickly. The month is coming to a close, and all is being readied for the upcoming nuptials. Prince Matthew and Princess Likeria are very much in love and have decided to live in the Kingdom of Likeria. Prince Matthew will be trained the Likerian way.

It is a rare and special union. Joy is brought into two kingdoms, and abundance will abound. The Likerians are special, mystical warriors who protect the worlds. The couple will want for nothing. The kingdoms will await the birth of the first child born of Likerian and Crystillian royals. Their children will be called Crystal Children, and they will be gifted in the ways of earth, healing, and communication.

Excitement is growing. The nuptials will be celebrated in a couple of days in the palace in Crystal City. The wagons of provisions are coming in from everywhere. As many wagons are being escorted from the Kingdom of Likeria as are coming from the Kingdom of Crystal City.

"Matthew! Matthew!" yells Princess Arabella. "You're home! I am so glad to see you!" She runs and hugs her brother. "How was it in the Kingdom of Likeria?"

"Just like here, Arabella. It is beautiful. When you come to visit after school, you will see it is just like home. Training to be a Likerian is another thing though. The training is like nothing I have ever known before. You will just love Princess Likeria. She will be like a big sister for you," says Prince Matthew.

"Well, let us hurry. Mother and Father are patiently waiting. Mother ordered all your favorites for lunch."

Prince Matthew and Princess Arabella hurry up the stairs of the palace to see the king and queen. Prince Matthew bursts through the doors of the dining room. His parents, with looks of great joy on their faces, stand as their son rushes to greet them. First, Prince Matthew throws his arms around his mother, Queen Amelia. The queen is so happy to see her son that she bursts into tears and says, "It is so good to see you, my son!"

"It is so good to see you too, Mother!" replies the excited prince as he hugs and lifts his mother off the ground.

Prince Matthew turns to his father. The king and prince embrace.

Everyone is happy to have the prince home. The news of the prince finding a bride has the whole kingdom buzzing with excitement.

King Gerald takes Prince Matthew by the arm and leads him from the room. "Son, I am very proud of the man that you have become."

"Thank you, Father."

"I have many questions."

"You have only to ask, Father."

"All right. How are the Likerians strategically placed? How is their energy wall functioning? Is the terrain the same as ours? And how about battle strategies? Similar?"

"Most things are similar, Father. Except when it comes to training to become a Likerian warrior—that is much different. We train using many techniques, most only known to the seers and oracles. This vision training is much more intense, and it is very interesting. One day when we have some spare time, we will talk more about it. For now we must concentrate on getting the wedding preparations in hand."

"Yes, let's talk with the staff and see where we are with the preparations. I will speak to the banquet staff, and you can check the grounds," states the anxious king. He watches his precious son bound out of the room in excitement over the upcoming nuptials.

CHAPTER 30

A few years have passed in Hagville. Sunlight streams through Prince Elgrin's bedroom window. The young prince lies on his bed, contemplating going to a school far away from the land he knows and loves. At least the prince is safe and knows that he will be attending school with his best friend, Hermie. It is only months now before he will have to leave Hagville. All he knows is that his new school is in a strange kingdom far from here. *It will be interesting*, the young prince thinks. He puts his hands under his head and closes his eyes to daydream of moments long past.

Prince Elgrin starts to giggle, remembering the antics of Hermie in the Dreary Forest. They were running, but he can't remember why.

All of a sudden, Hermie was gone. Yep, that's right, just gone. The prince remembers how he ran over to where Hermie had been and called out his name. The prince looked down at a bunch of rotten logs and noticed his friend's shoe lying there.

Hearing "Oooooooohhh," the agile prince climbed over the logs and saw his friend on the other side of the pile. His friend was on the ground, moaning and groaning. Prince Elgrin grabbed Hermie by the arm and helped him to his feet. He bursts out laughing even now, remembering.

"I was running after the little bluebird and looking high in the sky, when all of a sudden it was like I was hoisted in the air at about my knees. *Poof*, I was on the ground, and that is the last thing I remember until you grabbed my arm," Hermie had told him.

Bang! Bang! comes from Prince Elgrin's door, startling the young man out of his daydreams. "Yes?" yells the prince.

"Are you coming down for your breakfast?" asks his mother, Queen Hag.

"Yes, Mother, I will be right down."

Prince Elgrin throws his covers off and slides out of bed. As he is getting ready, something nags at him about the memory he has just had. *A bird? Hmmm, I don't remember a bird. Where did that come from? I will have to ask Hermie if he remembers a bird. A little bluebird? There is something very strange about that bird. Hmmm, I just can't place it. Maybe we will remember together what that bird means.*

The prince finishes getting ready and heads down the stairs to the kitchen for breakfast. As he enters, he is greeted by his mother and father already seated at the table.

"Good morning, Mother, Father," says the prince.

"Good morning, son," his father and mother reply in unison. Prince Elgrin grins to himself.

"My son, it is time to discuss the topic of your schooling. You are registered. Hermie is also registered, and you will both travel by boar carriage. The journey will be long, and Cook will pack you a lunch. When you are there, it is imperative that you listen to your instructors and your guard. As you are a prince, you are required to have a guard. Is that clear?" asks the king.

"Yes, Father, it is quite clear. I will need to gather my things for the journey. I will be ready when the time comes," says Prince Elgrin.

"That is good."

"I am off to see Hermie. We need to make a list so that we have all that we require for school."

The young prince finishes his breakfast, wipes his mouth, and leaves the kitchen after a wave to his mother and father.

Hermie is sitting on his bench, having his breakfast, when there is a knock at the door.

"Could you get the door, Trolby?" asks Edwina from the kitchen. She is carrying a huge pot of gruel to the fire.

Trolby gets up from the table, goes over to the door, and opens it. He sees Vincent, Hermie's pet rat, with a little scroll strapped to his back.

"Hmmmm," says Trolby. "I think it is for you, Hermie!"

Hermie gets up from the table and heads to the door. Bending, he retrieves the little scroll. Hermie reaches into his pocket and takes out a fat peanut for his favorite pet. Vincent grabs the tasty morsel and scampers back outside.

Trolby looks at Hermie as he unrolls the little scroll. Hermie just smiles, crumples the scroll, and puts it into his pocket.

"Well, who is it from, or do I need to guess?" Trolby laughs.

"Father, you know it is from Prince Elgrin. He is on his way over to make a list of what we should pack for our journey to the academy."

"All right, then, finish up your breakfast."

"Yes, Father," says Hermie. He swallows his last mouthful of gruel. He gathers his dishes from the table and hands them to his mother.

They hear a knock at the door. *It must be Prince Elgrin*, thinks Hermie as he goes to the door and opens it. Sure enough, it is his friend. Prince Elgrin walks in and pleasantries are exchanged. The two boys go through the kitchen and down the hall to Hermie's room.

Hermie blurts out, "Hey! Prince Elgrin, would you like to do this in the shed or at Soomie Swamp? I don't really feel like making our list here. Let's go outside and get some fresh air for a while."

"Good idea, Hermie. Let's go outside."

The two boys go to the window and crawl out, carrying a scroll and charcoal. They walk to the shed behind the house. Once inside the shed, the boys grab their stools and sit at a table to discuss the problem at hand—returning to school—which neither is too excited about. As long as they are both there, they know it will be very tolerable.

"Hermie, how do you think this term will be at the academy?" asks Prince Elgrin.

"I hope we can have a little fun there!" chortles Hermie with a wide grin.

"Oh, I don't think you have to worry about that. We have fun wherever we go. But it might be a little problematic with the guard that I will have to have with me."

"GUARD! You weren't kidding, then?" exclaims Hermie.

"Well, I am a prince. I do not go anywhere without a guard, at least until I come of age—I hope. Until then, we can try and lose him when we really want to have a little fun."

The boys make plans for school with much laughter and excitement.

"When do we go, Prince Elgrin?"

"In a couple of weeks, Father said."

"We haven't much time for fun at home, then."

"Want to walk over to Soomie Swamp and see all our friends for a swim? It would be great. We don't have a lot of time left before we have to pack."

"I was hoping you would say that. Sure, let's go. I already have my swimsuit on," replies Hermie.

The boys walk over to Soomie Swamp. The two romp the afternoon away, swimming and laughing with all of their friends.

CHAPTER 31

At Crystal City, the final stages of wedding preparations for Prince Matthew and Princess Likeria are being readied. The grounds are absolutely beautiful, with flowers in stands everywhere—roses, lilies, and gardenias. The smell is divine. Prince Matthew certainly hopes his bride will love it.

In the middle of the grounds is a beautiful gazebo curtained in sheer white linen. A red velvet carpet leads up to it. A solitary white podium stands at the end. On either side of the podium are huge arrangements of lilies, the most vibrant pink and white that can be found in all the kingdom. Pink is Princess Likeria's favorite color and lilies are her favorite flower. She will love them.

Flower pedestals line the walkway almost to the palace. The princess will appear from her royal carriage and be escorted down the carpet to the gazebo. There are rows upon rows of white chairs under huge pergolas so that all of the guests will be sheltered from the intense sun. Again, at the banquet area, huge pergolas have been built for the occasion. Sheer linens hang everywhere. The tables are lined with flowers and linens, ready for the banquet to be served for the happy couple. The kitchen staff is scurrying around with all the food preparation.

Everything happens on time. The guests arrive by the carriage load and are seated on the lovely white chairs by the gazebo, which are filling fast. The royals wait for the blowing of the horns announcing the arrival of the beautiful bride-to-be, Princess Likeria.

The horns begin to sound their low, hollow note, welcoming the royals as they step out of the palace and are escorted to the grounds by the guards. Prince Matthew walks behind King Gerald and Queen Amelia into the gazebo, where he will await his bride. Everyone is in position and everything is ready.

"There she is!" whispers one of the ushers. "She is beautiful!"

Prince Matthew looks down the royal red carpet and sees his bride being walked down the aisle by her father, King Olaf, and her mother, Queen Alexandria. Princess Likeria wears a long, flowing white gown, with layers and layers of pink taffeta and a beaded bodice. A white cape is attached to one shoulder, trailing past her gown on one side and attached to her wrist on the other side. Her necklace, a sapphire-and-diamond eagle encircled by a ring of raven-black diamonds: the Likerian emblem of the kingdom. She sports the same emblem on her neck, symbolizing the spiritual wisdom of the world. The emblem holds many secrets of the Kingdom of Likeria, all for the protection of the new world.

On her head, Princess Likeria wears a tiara made with the finest quality jewels. The princess is preceded by two little fairies sprinkling fairy dust in honor of the union of the prince and princess. Fairy dust is said to bring luck and pave the way for magic.

Prince Matthew waits with bated breath as his princess is walked to him by her father and mother. When they reach the prince, Queen Alexandria and King Olaf take their daughter's hand and place it in the hand of Prince Matthew. The king and queen kiss their daughter on the cheek and take their seats.

Smiling, Prince Matthew clasps Princess Likeria's hand. The ceremony lasts a short while. The newly married couple kiss for the first time, and the cheering begins.

The newlyweds walk back down the aisle, smiling and greeting everyone. Sirus is up above with several of his feathered and fairy friends, all holding a thin film of linen in their beaks. In the linen are thousands of gardenia petals just waiting to be released on the happy couple. Sirus motions, two of the sides are dropped, and a wonderful shower fall upon the couple, the crowd, and the aisle. The festivities are upon the royal couple: the musicians begin to play, and there is much merriment and joy in the kingdom.

Sirus, having done his duty for the bride and groom, flies over to the beautiful table where Princess Arabella sits with her parents, King Gerald and Queen Amelia. Sirus lands on the princess's shoulder.

"You were great, Sirus!" says Princess Arabella.

"Chirp! Chirp!" replies Sirus.

"Oh Sirus, you are so welcome. You and your friends did a great job."

The banquet begins. The guests eat the finest of foods from Crystal City and the Kingdom of Likeria. Everyone is having a fabulous time, singing, dancing, laughing, and dining. *What a wonderful celebration*, thinks the princess.

After many hours of celebrating, the happy couple leave for their wedding night. They make their way through the crowd, thanking all of the guests.

Finally! thinks Princess Arabella as the newly married couple reach the royal table. They hug and kiss Queen Amelia and King Gerald. Princess Arabella stands to greet her new sister-in-law. Princess Likeria bows slightly and hugs Princess Arabella. Prince Matthew also hugs his little sister, whispering in her ear that it soon will be her turn. Princess Arabella lets out a little laugh and smiles at her brother. "That is sooooo not going to happen any time soon." The prince lets out a hearty laugh.

A horn blows, signaling that it is time for Prince Matthew and Princess Likeria to leave. Their royal carriage is adorned with many flowers. The horses are draped with ribbons, crystals, and flowers as well. The couple performs an important ritual: Princess Likeria has Prince Matthew hoist her up a short way. She grabs her bouquet, closes her eyes, and tosses it high in the air behind her. As she throws it, Sirus swoops down and grabs the bouquet by a ribbon. He drops it right in the lap of Princess Arabella, who catches it. With a huge smile, she holds it up. Everyone cheers at the display.

All the maidens look at Princess Arabella, quite disappointed. The royal wedded couple look at her with a smile and twinkle in their eyes. They blow a kiss and wave at Princess Arabella. Then the royal newlyweds are whisked away to the Kingdom of Likeria, where they will reside until the time comes for them to take the throne from King Olaf and Queen Alexandria.

The happy Princess Arabella looks at the bouquet. The lilies are absolutely fabulous with all the ribbons.

"But wait, what is that?" says Princess Arabella. A very thin pink ribbon is in a loop inside the bouquet, just barely visible. She touches the ribbon and gives it a tug. To her amazement, there is a little scroll attached to the ribbon. Princess Arabella unties the ribbon from the scroll, and something falls to the table with a clink. She sees a silver ring, which she picks up and examines. The ring is decorated with the same emblem that Princess Likeria wears on her neck

The princess further examines the inside of the ring. To her amazement, she sees an engraving: *Arabella, our jewel.* She is quite taken aback, for she never expected a gift. She unrolls the scroll very carefully and reads:

Our dearest Arabella,

In the kingdom of Likeria, when a marriage takes place, a gift is given to someone special. When you need help of any kind, rub the ring in a counterclockwise motion on your finger, and you will be able to communicate with us. We are always near.

With much love,
Matthew and Likeria

Princess Arabella is so surprised by the unusual gift that she feels love for her new sister already. A secret magical ring! She is very excited. Going to the Academy of Etiquette and Epicure does not seem so daunting now that she can communicate with Prince

Matthew and Princess Likeria. The princess excitedly shows her parents her most special gift.

As morning arrives in Crystal City, Princess Arabella stretches and moans and groans. She pulls the covers over her eyes and tries to keep out the sunshine. Then there is a familiar *tap, tap* on the window. Sirus is patiently waiting for the princess to awaken from her slumber. Princess Arabella smiles and motions for Sirus to come in.

"Well, Sirus, now that the wedding is over, I will have to get ready for school," complains the princess.

"Chirp! Chirp!" says Sirus.

"I know, I know. I have to go to school. I know that I will meet many new friends and learn many new things, but did you know that Father is making me have two guards?"

"Chirp! Chirp!" says Sirus.

"I know it is for my own safety, but how will I ever have any fun?"

"Arabella, are you awake?" yells a servant.

"Yes! I am awake. I will be down soon for my breakfast," answers the princess, hurrying to get ready.

On her way out of her bedroom, she glances at her dresser and sees the ring that Princess Likeria and Prince Matthew gave her. She smiles. She takes the ring, puts it in a special box, and sets it in a secret drawer in the dresser.

Sirus follows Princess Arabella out of her room and down the stairs to the kitchen. Sirus is not allowed in the kitchen, so he makes a swift exit through a small stained-glass window in the entryway to wait for the princess.

Princess Arabella has breakfast and then goes off to help with the cleanup of the grounds. That is fun, with all the servants and other people helping.

The day is long but very fruitful. The grounds and the palace are cleaned up, and Arabella goes to her room. She gets ready for bed after packing and meeting the guards who will protect her on the journey in the morning.

I certainly don't appreciate Father making me have guards. I simply don't understand it. Really, what kind of trouble could a princess get into anyway? thinks the tired princess as she fades into sleep.

CHAPTER 32

In Hagville, the mood is quite solemn. Prince Elgrin is not looking forward to the military academy. But in a few days he and his friend will be on their way. It will be quite a journey.

All of a sudden there is pounding at the door. Startled, Prince Elgrin awakens from slumber. "Wh-what is it?" he croaks sleepily.

"It's your mother! Are you awake? I am coming in!"

"Yes, Mother, I am awake! Come in!"

"Elgrin, my son, you will be leaving tomorrow first thing in the morning. Hoodly will have the wild boar carriage waiting for you and Hermie. I just wanted to come in and say that I will miss you very much," says a teary-eyed Queen Hag.

"B-but tomorrow? That is so sudden. I thought I had more time. I need to pack! O h, Mother, I wish I had more time so I could pack slowly and not be so rushed."

"I would have thought that you were already packed, seeing as you have had two weeks to do it. Get up and get packed. I am sorry, son, but there is one more thing that I forgot to mention. Your father wants to send a guard with you, so you and your friend won't get into trouble on the way there. The journey is long. Get dressed and come down for breakfast. At least have a quick bite of something, and then you can finish your packing. The scroll with the list of school items is on your desk. The necessary scrolls, charcoal, and supplies are in a box on your desk as well. You need to pack anything else you want to take with you, including staffs, swords and other weaponry," says Queen Hag, and she exits the room.

She enters the dining room to find her husband, King Minos, already seated at the table. "Did you speak with Elgrin?" he asks.

"Yes, I stopped by his room on the way down. He will be joining us shortly. He is not very happy at the mention of having a guard—and there he is now," says Queen Hag. Prince Elgrin bolts through the kitchen door.

"Good morning, son," says King Minos.

"Good morning, Father, Mother," says Prince Elgrin as he nods to his parents.

The young prince is served gruel and quail eggs. Cook sets milk in front of him. Prince Elgrin gobbles down his breakfast and gives each parent a kiss on the cheek before he runs out the door.

With much to do, the prince heads out of the castle. He needs to see Hermie before they leave the next morning. They must discuss every possible thing they may need at the military academy. Instead of taking the tram, however, the prince decides to take the extra time to walk through the treetop city, wanting to clear his head. A little walk will be quite refreshing.

Prince Elgrin makes his way through the winding walkways in the treetops and sees all sorts of people going to and from work and shops. The smells coming from the bakery are divine. He stops in and gets a couple pastries for Hermie and himself. *We can have a quiet moment before we have to finish packng*, thinks Prince Elgrin.

After walking for what seems like an hour, he sees the hovel of his friend. Prince Elgrin walks up to the door, being careful not to step on Vincent the rat, and knocks on the door. He hears footsteps, and Hermie opens the door.

"It's Prince Elgrin, Ma!" Hermie calls back over his shoulder. "We are going to the shed. We need to check our list of school supplies. Prince Elgrin says we leave tomorrow morning. Back soon!"

Hermie and Prince Elgrin scurry off to their secret clubhouse. It is just the shed behind the house, but it is their private sanctuary.

The boys walk in and sit at the makeshift table. Prince Elgrin gives a pastry to Hermie. They eat their treat and chat about the upcoming journey.

When the boys are done eating the pastries, they give all of the crumbs to Vincent. Then they discuss all the items they need at school. In a short time, they are ready to finish the packing and prepare for the arduous journey ahead. The boys go their separate ways.

There is a lot to do. Prince Elgrin hopes the servants will pack all that he has instructed them to pack. He is going to pack all of his special treasures—or at least a few to take with him. He is very excited for the trip. It grows late, and he turns in for the night. Sleep does not come easily. Thoughts of the next morning are swimming around in his head.

CHAPTER 33

*B*ang! *Bang*! *Bang*! Princess Arabella is startled awake by a loud banging at her door.

"Princess Arabella! Are you awake?" bellows one of the servants.

"Yes! I am awake. What is it? What is wrong?" answers the drowsy princess.

"Your breakfast is ready, and the king and queen are downstairs waiting for you!"

"But it is still dark!" she exclaims.

"The horses are saddled and waiting. Your guards are on standby at the kitchen, waiting to take you to school, remember?"

"Oh my, yes, school. I will be right down," replies the princess.

A few minutes later, the princess bounds down the stairs into the kitchen, dressed in her riding gear.

"Did you forget that today is the day you leave for the academy?" her father asks.

"I am sorry, Father, but I could not get to sleep last night. I am ready to go now. I see the servants have my horse saddled. And of course the guards are waiting for me. But two! Do I really need two guards, Father?"

"Yes. We have gone over this many times, my dear, and the guards stay! Are we clear?"

"Yes, Father. I guess you should introduce me to them," says the princess.

King Gerald summons the guards. The door opens and in walk the two guards. One is tall and thin with white hair, a bit of a moustache, and spectacles. He has quite an accent and is kind of funny. *He might just be okay*, thinks the princess. *Oh, and the other one isn't so funny.* He is shorter, a robust guard with no hair and round little spectacles. *All business, this one*, thinks the princess.

"Arabella, I would like you to meet your guards, Captain Mazelle and General Frank." King Gerald points to each of the guards as he speaks. Princess Arabella bows to each. "The princess shall be out shortly," states the king. He nods to the guards, and they turn and go back outside.

The princess finishes her breakfast and hugs each of her parents before walking out the door. She dons her jacket, heading down the huge staircase. One of the guards holds her horse for her.

"Captain Mazelle at your service, Princess."

"Thank you, Captain Mazelle," says the princess. Captain Mazelle helps her mount her steed before turning and mounting his own horse.

"Princess Arabella, I am General Frank. I have been instructed by your father to escort you to the academy and shadow all of your movements. Is that clear?" asks the very stern general.

"Yes, sir," replies the princess.

The trio begin to ride, the princess between the two guards. The journey will take them into the Emerald Forest and then through Mystic Mountain, where, after a day's ride, they will come to the Academy of Etiquette and Epicure in the Kingdom of Wallace.

CHAPTER 34

Prince Elgrin is awake well before it is time to rise. He is all packed, and his luggage is loaded into the carriage. He sits patiently, waiting to go down and have his last breakfast before the adventure of a lifetime.

Finally! Prince Elgrin thinks as he hears the footsteps of the little troll coming down the hall to call him for breakfast.

The prince quickly hides behind the door and waits. *Knock, knock, knock.* Silence. Prince Elgrin looks at the doorknob and sees it turning, just as he knew it would. The door opens, and the little troll rounds the frame.

"*Booooooooo!*" rings out through the hall.

The little troll jumps a couple of feet into the air and screams, flailing his arms. He lands with a thud, his matted green hair still flopping.

Prince Elgrin buckles over, laughing so hard that he is crying. He shakes the troll to see if he is okay.

The troll bounds up in a huff and screeches, "I certainly won't miss that!" He storms off.

Prince Elgrin slowly gets up off the floor and proceeds down to the kitchen for his breakfast. Still smiling, he bursts into the kitchen.

"Good morning, son!" yell Queen Hag and King Minos.

"Good morning, Mother, Father," replies Prince Elgrin.

The royals sit and have their breakfast while talking about school. Suddenly there is a loud knock at the door. The three royals turn and see two little troll guards at the doorway. They announce the arrival of the carriage and the guard who will accompany the prince and his friend to the military academy. They abruptly bow, turn, and leave with a bang of the door.

Prince Elgrin stands and bids his parents farewell with a tender embrace. Once in the queen's carriage, the prince just sits and thinks. The carriage rolls forward to pick up his friend Hermie. This is going to be a great adventure.

The boars come to a snorting stop. The little troll gets off the carriage and opens the door for Hermie, who has been waiting by the tram. Hermie steps up and sits down beside Prince Elgrin. The little troll shuts the door, throws Hermie's bags on the carriage, and gets back onto the carriage. The pair is finally off on their journey to the military academy.

It will take several days to reach their destination. The two settle in for the long ride. They must once again traverse the Dreary Forest. It will be quite a harrowing journey for the adventurous pair.

CHAPTER 35

The royal trio has been riding all day. They near a quaint meadow at the base of Mystic Mountain. Princess Arabella hears the rushing of water. She is quite bored with the journey so far. She decides to stir things up a bit and suddenly veers off the path. She gallops at great speed away from General Frank and Captain Mazelle. Stunned by the actions of the princess, General Frank waves his arm and roughly turns his horse to follow the princess. Captain Mazelle hastily turns and follows.

Princess Arabella turns her head to see how far her guards are behind her. Out of nowhere, she is thrown from her horse and plummets down, down, down into a deep pool of water.

It is very dark. She treads water until her eyes adjust, and she sees that she has fallen into some kind of well. There is sand a short distance away. She swims over to it and walks up the sandy area. She keeps walking to a wall. There is a torch in a metal holder mounted on the stone. She feels around and, in a small opening in the wall, finds some matches. She strikes one against the stone, and the match flares. The princess lights the torch; luckily it catches fire right away. She looks around in awe. She walks around the pool of water and lights all the torches. Then she hears something.

"Ayyeeeeeee!" *Splash*!

Princess Arabella turns around, and there in the very spot where she landed minutes before is Captain Mazelle. Princess Arabella buckles over in laughter and says, "Mazelle, how did you get here? Never mind. I know how you got here, but how did you find me?"

"It's *Captain* Mazelle to you, young miss. When you bolted from the group, we were forced to separate and look for you. I saw your horse on the same path that I was on. All of a sudden, my horse reared and threw me off! So here I am, and now we have to find a way out of here." Captain Mazelle, looking around, asks, "What is this place?" He trips and falls to the ground.

Still laughing, Princess Arabella goes over and lends a hand. Grumbling and dusting himself off, Captain Mazelle straightens out and goes to the wall to see if he can tell where they are.

"Maybe there is a hidden doorway," suggests the curious princess.

"I hope so," says Captain Mazelle.

Captain Mazelle and Princess Arabella run their hands all over the walls, pushing and examining, trying to find some sort of opening. They work at this for what seems like an hour until—

"Mazellie, I think I found something!" yells the excited princess.

"I am coming, Princess!" yells Captain Mazelle, breaking into a run. In his accident-prone way, with his odd camel run and tall, lanky frame, he falls. This time he falls headfirst into the sand. Not hurt, but spitting sand, he gets up and hobbles over to the snickering princess. She is trying to pry open what she thinks is a doorway.

Meanwhile, General Frank, quite frantic, races back to the palace with two lone horses. Not only has Princess Arabella gone missing, but so has Captain Mazelle. This surely cannot be good.

How am I to tell the king of the disaster? thinks the worried General Frank as he nears the palace.

King Gerald is at the door. He motions to the general to follow him into the meeting room. The pair proceeds inside to plan what they are going to do next.

CHAPTER 36

"How long did you say the ride is? If we don't stop soon, I think I am going to be sick. It is so bumpy! I don't think that I have touched the seat for more than five minutes!" says Hermie.

"I don't think it is much farther. I can see a clearing in the valley, just before Turffs Ridge. That is where we are to spend the night. In the morning, I am afraid, we have to continue on the wild boars. They will be saddled and ready for us after breakfast. It will be a two-day ride. We will have a guide and a four-day supply of food, so we should be all right," advises Prince Elgrin.

The clearing is not far away. It is getting dark. They slowly approach a lake. It is a moonlit night, and the reflection on the water is magical. The convoy decides to stop. They want to stretch their legs and then look at the beauty of the reflection of the moon on the lake. Everything is very still.

There is a strange fog rolling in. It is a purple fog. The boys stand up and watch. A picture forms in the fog, slowly becoming clearer and clearer. It is an image of a girl with light-colored hair done in braids. She is dressed in some sort of uniform and cape, like a royal would wear. Then, as quickly as the fog rolled in, it fades out.

There is something about her, the prince thinks, and with that thought she is gone.

Prince Elgrin looks at Hermie. His friend looks back at him with an expression of utter shock. Throwing his arms up in the air, Hermie says in a loud whisper, "What the heck was that?"

The little guard walks over. Hearing what the boys are taking about, he says, "Boys, you are not the first to see a vision in the fog. There have been many before you. If you have questions in your heart, the fog answers them. It takes much searching within to decipher the fog. This place is called the Waters of Vision. This night has been special. Now, let's get going. We have to set up camp."

The convoy heads out. In no time at all, they are setting up camp and preparing supper. Shortly after, their lights go out one by one. The boars are snug, tethered to big albertroken trees. The last puffs of smoke come from the fire pit. All is quiet in the camp. Sleep comes easily.

CHAPTER 37

"Pull!" yells the princess. Her fingers are almost white as she squeezes them into the small gap in the rocks. Captain Mazelle has his thin fingers in the gap as well. The pair cannot get their fingers in far enough to make an effort at pulling the door open.

"We need a strong stick or knife or something sturdier and thinner to pry the door open with. I think it will open if we can find something. This is our only way out, Princess. We must find something!" commands the worried Captain Mazelle.

The pair looks around their prison surroundings, stopping to pick up rocks and things, looking for the right-size tool to open the door—the only door that can possibly lead them out of this place. The only door that—

A bloodcurdling scream echoes through the well.

The princess pivots around to face the pool of water. Captain Mazelle is standing pinned against the wall, and there is a creature—a gigantic snake! It is a long, huge, green-and-blue-speckled snake with a big head. Oddly, it wears glasses and speaks. Hissing loudly, it asks Captain Mazelle questions. "Hissssssssss, who are you? Hissssssssss, why are you here? Hissssss."

Captain Mazelle is paralyzed with fear. Unable to speak, he slowly goes limp and plunks to the ground. The snake slithers toward the fallen captain.

Princess Arabella runs to the captain and yells, "Mazelle! Mazelle! Wake up! Wake up!"

The snake rears his head and turns to see Princess Arabella trying to wake her friend. "Hissssssss! Who are you? Hisssssss," asks the snake.

"I … I am Princess Arabella of the Kingdom of Crystal City. And who, may I ask, are you?" stammers the frightened princess.

"Hissssssssss. A princess, you say? From Crystal City? Well, Princess Arabella, my name is Norbert. Hisssssssss. It has been many a moon since I saw humans here. Why have you come?" hisses Norbert.

"I got lost, and my horse bucked me off, and I landed in your pool of water. Captain Mazelle, sorry to say, met the same fate as I did. Now we are just trying to get out of here!" cries Princess Arabella.

"Hisssssssss. That may be difficult, for I am the keeper of the Mystical Cavern. There are many doors in the cavern. You must choose correctly to leave. If you choose incorrectly, you will become my dinner. Hissssssssss."

"Your dinner? I don't think so! Norbert, just tell me what we need to do to find the right door to get out of here!"

Captain Mazelle begins to stir. "Mazelle! Mazelle!" yells the princess as she starts shaking Captain Mazelle.

The groggy captain opens his eyes. "Wha …? Where am I?"

"Mazelle, did you forget? Just look around! I am sure you will remember. I would also like to introduce Norbert to you."

Captain Mazelle's eyes grow saucer large, and he once again faints. Princess Arabella shakes her head, runs over to the pool of water, and scoops some water into her cupped hands. She walks over to Captain Mazelle and throws the water right in his face.

He sputters and coughs. "What was that for?" he yells.

"It's time to wake up and look around! You have met Norbert the snake, who will, I hope, lead us out of here. Father and General Frank are going to be frantic if we don't get out of here and get to the academy," replies the princess.

"Hissssssssss. Did you say the academy? Would that be the Academy of Etiquette and Epicure?" hisses Norbert.

"Why, yes. How did you know?" asks Princess Arabella.

"I am a friend of Headmistress Vale. That is all I can tell you for the moment. And I will take you to the academy as a favor to Headmistress Vale!" says Norbert.

"As a favor? Headmistress Vale? How do you know her?" asks the princess.

"Hissssssssssss. All I can tell you is that I am in allegiance with Princess Likeria and Prince Matthew of the Kingdom of Likeria."

"Prince Matthew! Princess Likeria! They are my brother and sister-in-law! They were just married in the Kingdom of Crystal City. Why are you helping them? Who are you?" quizzes the suspicious princess.

"Hisssssssss. All I can tell you is that I am Norbert, Keeper of the Secret Waters. There are many things in this world that you will not understand, Princess Arabella. You must believe. You are a seeker, a seeker of truths, truths that have been hidden. Princess Likeria and your brother are Keepers of the Worlds, and it is imperative that nothing stand in their way of keeping the worlds safe. I shall help you in ways that I am capable of. That is all that I can tell you. One more thing: if you ever require assistance in the future, I shall be available. We must leave now!"

"You must tell me more. We cannot leave yet. I have many questions!" retorts Princess Arabella.

Norbert slithers over to Captain Mazelle, who is getting up from his fainting spell. Still a little in shock, Captain Mazelle looks at the princess and then back at the huge snake. Princess Arabella grabs him by the arm.

"All right, get on!" hisses Norbert.

"Get on? Get on what? Aren't you slimy and slithery? How will we stay on you? We will just slide off. And how will we get out of here anyway?" asks Captain Mazelle.

"Hissssssssssss, just get on and squeeze your legs around me."

Sure enough, the lost pair straddle the snake and, miraculously, it is as if they are sitting on saddles. There's even a little horn to hang on to, molded right into Norbert's back.

"Hisssssss. Ready? Hang on. When we reach the water, just hold your breath. It will only be for a few secondssssssss," hisses Norbert.

"Hang on! Here we go, Mazelle! Woo-hoo!"

Norbert and his two passengers start the journey, slithering into the sand around the pool and then into the waters of the Mystical Cavern.

"Hissssss. Hold your breaths, humansssssss!"

The trio is in the water, going down and then up. They hold their breaths for what seems like hours. Princess Arabella can see light through the water. They are coming closer to the light.

Splashhhh! The trio is out of the water now and slithering at a quick pace into a nearby forest. Norbert begins to slow down. Princess Arabella and Captain Mazelle seem to slide right off his back. They land with a bump in a jumbled heap. The pair rise and shake themselves off. Then they start to walk. They haven't a clue as to where they are.

"Do you smell it, Mazelle?" asks Princess Arabella.

"Yes, Princess, I smell it. Smoke. There must be someone close by. But be careful. We do not know where we are or if we can trust Norbert. He might have dropped us off to be someone else's dinner."

"Well, I think that we can trust Norbert. He belongs to the Kingdom of Likeria. He is here to help Princess Likeria and Prince Matthew."

"Look!" Captain Mazelle points.

There, just barely visible, they can see smoke rising from the thick forest. As the pair walks on, a tall, thin man with red hair, wearing some sort of uniform, comes into view. He is walking back and forth. His head is down and his hands are clasped behind his back. The closer the pair get, the easier it is to hear his mumbling as he paces.

"Hello!" yells Princess Arabella.

The startled man jumps and turns. He walks to the royal pair.

Captain Mazelle has to keep the princess safe. "What do you want?" he asks.

"I am Francois, assistant to Headmistress Vale from the Academy of Etiquette and Epicure, at your service. It is about time that you got here. I have been waiting hours for your arrival. I was glad to hear Norbert had you and not the—" Francois stops short.

"Not the—not the what? Or should I say who?" questions Princess Arabella.

"It does not matter now, Princess. We must get you safely to the academy and notify your father that you and your guard have arrived safely via a different route. Hurry, we must go. The academy is not far. Your things will be here shortly," says Francois.

The new trio trudges through the forest. It is a long journey. They stop and sit on a log to rest a while. Francois opens his big leather satchel and pulls out some mulberries. Princess Arabella and Captain Mazelle gobble up most of the mulberries and wash them down with a little juice from Francois's bag. Nourished and refreshed, they once again set out for the academy.

Passing through a meadow, they notice a huge, commanding structure at the top of the hill on the other side of the meadow.

"Is that the academy, Francois?" asks the princess.

"Yes, it is. We must not dillydally, as the light is waning. Won't be long now and you can wash up and change for dinner. Headmistress Vale is expecting you both," answers Francois.

They enter the large gates. They look around the massive grounds. They walk past fountains, down a walk, and into the school building through the main entrance hall. The academy is huge.

"This way, Princess Arabella," instructs Francois. They climb a long spiral staircase, walk down a long hall, turn a corner, climb another set of stairs, and pass more rooms. Finally they stop.

"Here is your room, Princess," says Francois, grabbing the handle of the big oak door and pushing it open.

Francois leads them into the huge main room of her dorm. It has all the comforts of home. A huge fireplace in the center is surrounded by big, comfy couches. Lots of windows line the room on one side. On the other walls are three doors. One leads to the bedroom of the princess, and the others to quarters for her guards.

Francois opens the doors to their respective rooms. Princess Arabella goes into hers and is amazed at how the furnishing are close to her own at home, right down to the fireplace in the corner. It is a perfect replica of her bedroom, bathroom, dressing area, and lounge, all in a single space.

The princess's things have arrived, and the servants are hauling them in. The guards' bags are being hauled into their rooms as well.

"Headmistress Vale expects you in an hour for dinner. Your bath is drawn and your luggage is here. Clean up and rest a while, and you will be called," instructs Francois.

Captain Mazelle secures the rooms.

CHAPTER 38

Back at Prince Elgrin's camp, a little fog hangs over the lake. Deep in the valley, there is a chill in the air. The camp begins to stir. One of the guides gets a fire going. The other is packing up his tent.

Prince Elgrin and Hermie emerge from their tents, folding their arms and grabbing their shoulders in the brisk morning air. Breakfast is not ready yet. The boys take a walk to the Waters of Vision and speak of the events of the night before.

"Do you remember or can you think of anything that might lead us to that girl?" asks Hermie.

"No. I could hardly sleep, thinking about it, but I had the strangest dream. You and I were chasing something in the Dreary Forest. I don't know … It was strange though," replies the chilled prince.

"Prince Elgrin! Prince Elgrin!"

The guides are yelling that breakfast is ready. The boys go back to the camp They sit and talk with the guides while they eat their breakfast.

All packed, the troops saddle the wild boars and continue on their way up the mountain. The terrain is quite treacherous. Narrow, winding trails switch up and then down the slope. The day is long. The troop is finally almost down the other side, but the light is fading once more and everyone is hungry, So they are forced to look for a spot to make camp.

They veer off the well-beaten path. After a short ride, the guide sees a small glade. The group rides that way, and then everyone dismounts to set up camp.

Prince Elgrin and Hermie need to stretch their legs. They go for a walk in the trees. A short distance from the camp, Hermie spots something. "Hey Prince Elgrin, come over here! I think I found something!"

Prince Elgrin dashes over to his friend, who is standing next to an opening in the face of the mountain.

"Well? What do you think? Should we go in? We need some light," says Hermie.

"Of course we should go in. I have a light in my bag," replies the excited Prince Elgrin. He runs back to camp and gets his bag, trying not to be noticed by his guards. He sneaks back to the cave, where Hermie is impatiently waiting for him. Prince Elgrin rummages in his bag and grabs a small torch from the side pocket. He strikes a match and lights it. The two boys crouch down, holding the torch in front of them, trying to see what is inside the cave. The light makes cobwebs shine. The two enter the cave.

"This isn't a cave. It's some sort of passageway!" exclaims Prince Elgrin.

"Let's keep going and see where it leads. The guards are still setting up, and they have to make a fire and cook. We have time, Prince," says Hermie.

Prince Elgrin looks at Hermie and smiles. The two walk for nearly five minutes. Then they see a room with eight sides. There is a doorway on each side. Prince Elgrin sees strange markings on the floor that branch out to each doorway. The boys follow the markings to the center of the room. They hold the torch high to see as much as they can.

"What is this place?" asks Hermie.

"I have no idea. I have never heard or read of such a place," answers the puzzled Prince Elgrin. "But I do think that we had better return to camp. Do you remember which way we came in, Hermie?"

"I think it is this way." Hermie points. Then he studies the eight pathways leading out from the center of the room. "Hmmmm, no. Maybe it's this one." He turns. "Or is it this one?" He stops and sits in the center of the pathways.

Prince Elgrin takes a breath and holds the torch over his head. He takes three steps back and turns this way and that way. He points to a pathway and grabs his friend's hand to boost him up. They start down the chosen pathway. All is silent. Have they chosen correctly? They could be lost forever.

The hungry prince and his friend hurry out of the cavern opening. They have chosen correctly.

The young men see the smoking fire of the camp. The guards are waving, summoning the two for some food and much-needed sleep. Tomorrow they will be at the military academy—how exciting! The two friends hurry to the camp for nourishment and sleep, vowing to never say a word about what they have seen.

"Where were the two of you?" barks the guard.

"We just went for a walk to stretch our legs."

"You must have gone a long way. We were calling you for some time. Prince Elgrin, you're not to be wandering around, or a guard will accompany you at all times. If that is what you want, one more time and you will get it. Is that clear?" shouts the guard.

"Yes, sir! It will not happen again," replies the prince.

The boys sheepishly eat their supper in silence and soon retire to their tents. Prince Elgrin tosses and turns most of the night. He dreams of the beautiful girl he has seen in the fog. He knows her, but how?

Prince Elgrin is being shaken awake.

"Prince! Prince! Get up! You have to come and look outside. You have to see it! It is gigantic! Hurry!" yells Hermie as he scrambles out of the prince's tent.

Prince Elgrin throws his blankets aside. He puts on some clothes and runs out of the tent. "What in the world is going on, Hermie? What is all this fuss about?" he asks.

That's when he sees it. It is massive: a stone building so huge it looks like it would swallow up the whole village of Hagville. The two boys look at each other and then, with twinkles in their eyes, eat their breakfasts.

Packing is quick this morning, as everyone can see how close they are to the academy. Onward! The troop reaches the academy gates, and a guard jumps off his boar and goes to where the gatekeeper sits. The two have a discussion, arms flailing. The gate opens. The guard mounts his wild boar, and they set off to the steps of the main building. They pass the pristine grounds, stables, and many other buildings.

The main building is majestic in stature. It is built of gray rock from the mountain. *Interesting,* thinks Prince Elgrin. He examines the wonderful architecture of the building. It has cathedral windows and turrets, which remind him of a castle of yore and the silly little tales the servants used to whisper about. The grounds are gigantic. Some people are milling about. Horses can be seen in pens at the stables. It is quite an impressive place.

Creak! The massive stone door slowly opens. On the other side is a rather short gentleman, about four feet tall, wearing tall boots, black pants, and a vest. Over this uniform is a red cape, attached to his shirt with big silver buttons. He is quite a staunch-looking fellow. He approaches the group.

"Good day, y'all. My name is Lord Hoaggie, and I am the director of the academy," he says, nodding to his audience. The group acknowledges with their own nods. "Ah, and y'all must be Prince Elgrin."

"Yes, and this is my friend Hermie," replies Prince Elgrin with a slight bow.

"Well, gentlemen, it is time to come in. My assistant, Brennie, will show you to your quarters."

The group walks inside with the guide. The guards bring in the supplies and baggage. Once inside, the group is introduced to Brennie. She is not quite what they expected. She is as short as Lord

Hoaggie and is dressed in a red uniform and little hat. Her hair is a bit matted, and she wears little round glasses as well. *She doesn't look so scary*, thinks Hermie.

"Chop, chop! Get a move on!" barks Brennie, slapping her gloves into her hand.

Brennie leads them down hallways, up stairs, and finally to their quarters. With the last of the students here, she can go back to her office and do the paperwork.

When everyone is settled into their respective rooms, the prince hears a knock at his door. He is just finishing unpacking and hopes that the knocker is not Brennie. He is happy when he does not see Brennie on the other side of the door, but Hermie. Prince Elgrin opens the door and invites Hermie in. The pair sit on a large brown sofa and talk about the past few days—of what they have seen and the adventures that lie ahead. And they laugh and laugh.

There is a loud pounding at the door that makes the two friends jump. This time, to their chagrin, it *is* Brennie. She has come to announce dinner and a gathering of all students in half an hour.

Since Hermie and the prince have already finished unpacking, they decide to take a little walk and explore before they meet in the great hall for dinner. They check out the school, looking into every doorway that is not locked. The classrooms are large. Some have desks, and some have experiment tables and stools.

The half hour is almost up, and the boys do not want to be late for dinner at the great hall. They quicken their pace and catch up to other students going down the hall. A mass of students fills the great room. The boys enter and look around for seats. They see signs on the tables. A sign that reads *First Year* is on the table to their far right, and they walk past it to their table. The commotion continues for a few minutes as everyone gets into their seats.

Load Hoaggie gives a brief introduction and welcome speech. Dinner is served. The room is silent while the students eat. After the last one has finished dessert, the students are taken on a tour of the school. The new classes will start in the morning. The two boys are signed up for Captain Milligan's workshop on weaponry.

Tour over, the boys are tired. They decide to go to their quarters and get some sleep. Good-night pleasantries are spoken, and the boys turn in for the night.

Sleep does not come easily to the prince. He tosses and turns most of the night. He can't get the image of the girl out of his mind. Every time he closes his eyes, he sees her. But who is she? She seems familiar, but he cannot remember why. He must try, but he must also get some sleep.

Am I dreaming? thinks Prince Elgrin as he looks toward his closet. There seems to be a light coming from under the door. He gets up, puts on his robe, and goes over to the closet, a little apprehensive about what he might find. He grabs the doorknob and takes a breath. Then he pulls the door open.

To the prince's surprise, there is nothing there. The light is emanating from his own little tree-trunk box. It certainly is bright. Prince Elgrin opens the box by twisting the lid, and finds a strange thing—a flower, a gardenia—is the source of the glowing light.

"Strange," Prince Elgrin thinks out loud. "Why would this flower glow?"

The prince closes the lid and goes back to his bed, where he snuggles in and drifts off to sleep.

CHAPTER 39

Princess Arabella steps from her bathtub and dries herself off. "Mmm, that was wonderful! With a little nap and a soak, I feel like a new person, ready to meet with Headmistress Vale—and a yummy dinner, I hope, ha-ha," Princess Arabella says.

Now ready, she leaves her bedroom. In the living area is Captain Mazelle, seated on the sofa, reading some papers. He looks up with his big blue eyes and, scowling, says, "Well, it is about time you came out. Francois should be here any minute to take us down to dinner with Headmistress Vale."

"Oh, Mazelle, everything is going to be fine," says Princess Arabella with a coy smile.

"Fine? Fine? Just because we arrived here with little incident, that does not at all mean fine! What happens when General Frank gets here? He is with your father right now, and I am sure he will not be in such a splendid mood. You had better be on your best behavior, Princess. Do you understand?" Captain Mazelle says gruffly.

"Yes, Mazelle. I get it. I will be on my best behavior when General Frank gets here. But until then, I want to go and explore the grounds!"

"You are not going anywhere, young lady! Francois will be down shortly to take us to dinner," Mazelle reminds her.

Bang! Bang! Bang!

"There he is the door now. Make sure you are ready!"

Captain Mazelle opens the door and invites Francois in. After a brief exchange, they follow Francois down to the great room for dinner.

The huge double doors of the great room are opened by a couple of servants, who bow as the royals enter the great room. The great room is massive, as is everything here. There must be hundreds of round tables with fancy tablecloths glimmering with shining silver. The dishes and glassware are exquisite. The servants pull out chairs for the ladies. It is a very formal dinner. Thank goodness Princess Arabella is royalty and knows about all of this finery.

Mazelle, on the other hand, is not. The princess helps Mazelle with his fork etiquette.

Headmistress Vale rises from her chair, lifts her glass, and welcomes her new students as well as those who have come back. "Welcome, students! I am pleased to see that you all have made the journey from your respective kingdoms. It is going to be an exciting season with the new classes added to the schedule. The most exciting is nature studies with Professor Graemee. He has the highest educational standing in his field. Professor Graemee will be teaching you the art of herbology—the identification of plants and their uses, especially the making of tinctures and salves."

Professor Graemee is of medium stature. He is peaceful-looking, but, as the princess knows, looks can be deceiving. He has a thick mane of short, curly, graying hair. He wears round glasses and carries an umbrella. He is quite a distinguished-looking fellow in his academy uniform.

"In addition to Professor Graemee, may I also introduce to you Madam Juditha, teacher of the great mystery. In her class, you will learn the history of our world and the worlds within."

Professor Juditha is the exact opposite of Professor Graemee—a short, stout sort. She wears her hair in a bun on top of her head. Her uniform is similar to Professor Graemee's: the same royal blue, only with a skirt. Her cape hides her stout form. She has stick legs and big clunky heels on her shoes. *She is so cute!* thinks the princess. *She kind of reminds me of a wise old owl.*

There is a great *crack* as Professor Juditha's walking stick hits the desk. Everyone sits up straighter in their chairs, paying the utmost attention to this new professor. The small group at Princess Arabella's table already knows that they do not like this teacher. Princess Arabella hopes that this opinion is wrong. This professor could spoil all of her fun.

Headmistress Vale continues to list off the professors at the academy. There is Dame Seanna, who teaches etiquette. There is Madam Lee, who is mistress of the fine art of cookery. Her dishes are known across the land. The newest of the professors is Professor Karlita, who teaches identification of the magical creatures in the mystic realms. There are many more professors who do not interest the princess, such as the Professor Wilhelmina, instructor of personal beauty; Professor Sulee, instructor of self-defense; and of course Professor Daniela, the linguistics instructor.

Headmistress Vale finishes her speech and takes the new students on a tour of the facility. She wishes them a good term. The group breaks up into smaller clusters of students. They slowly meet and mingle, then disperse to their rooms for the night.

It has been a great day for the princess, and tomorrow will begin a wonderful school term. With that thought, the princess says good night to Mazelle and they go into their separate quarters. Princess Arabella falls into a deep and peaceful sleep.

CHAPTER 40

Months have passed since Prince Elgrin entered the military academy. Some of his classes are difficult, and others come easy to the young prince. Soon it will be time to return to Hagville for the holidays. Prince Elgrin and Hermie have learned a lot about history, pen and pestle handling, weaponry, and survival skills. They cannot wait to see their friends and catch them up on the antics at the military academy. There will be many stories to tell.

Scrolls have been delivered and received, and it is time for celebration at the last dinner before the students pack up and leave the school for a few weeks. Upon returning, the studies will resume with the same intensity.

Clang! Clang! The gigantic dinner bell rings, and the students from every wing are on their way to the great room. They file in and go to their respective seats. Lord Hoaggie is standing at the podium, waiting to speak to his students.

"Evenin', y'all. This, as you know, will be the last dinner at the school until y'all return in a few weeks. I do hope y'all will enjoy your brief holiday and return safe and sound for the rest of the school season. All the roads in the kingdom will be cleared for those whose journey is lengthy. See y'all when you get back! Enjoy your dinner!"

Lord Hoaggie waves at the students and sits down as the meal begins to be served. The staff and students fill their plates with stuffed buzzard, which is divine, as are all the side dishes.

Chatter commences as students are finishing up. Clusters of students congregate here and there, wishing each other well. Prince Elgrin and Hermie join the well-wishers for a while and then make their way to their quarters to pack. It is so exciting to be going home after all these months.

Prince Elgrin is sitting on his bed, packing, when again he sees a light in his closet. He gets up to investigate. The light is coming from his special tree-trunk box, as before. He opens it. To his amazement, he finds the gardenia as fresh and lush-looking as the day it was picked. Prince Elgrin is rather puzzled at the flower, as he does not know where it has come from. Again, it seems to be familiar, but he just can't place it.

It will come to me, thinks the prince. *Maybe I will ask Mother and Father. They may know. But no time to waste now. I have to finish packing. Woo-hoo! We are going home and will get to see our families. It will be nice to take a break from studies and have a little fun at Soomie Swamp with our friends.*

Well, I guess I am all packed. It is getting late, and I must get to sleep. Morning will come quickly, and I can hardly wait!

The prince sets his bags close to the door and sits on his bed, contemplating how the days of traveling will be. He gets ready for bed and crawls under the covers for a good sleep.

CHAPTER 41

The many months drag on at the Academy of Etiquette and Epicure. Princess Arabella is ready for adventure. With the presence now of General Frank as well as Captain Mazelle, the young princess has been diligently working at her studies and not goofing off. King Gerald is very proud of his daughter for continuing her studies in such a way. There are not any bad reports, even from General Frank. King Gerald meets monthly with General Frank in addition to leaders from many other kingdoms on matters of world safety—and, of course, to play a round of king's ransom, a wonderful card game enjoyed by all kingdom leaders.

Princess Arabella runs ever so quickly up the stairs and down the hall, turning this way and that to get to her room and pack for the holidays. The students received word after their supper that they must pack, for they will have a few weeks of break before studies start up again. The young princess is very excited to see her friends at Crystal City again.

Princess Arabella opens the door to her room and looks around. She has beaten Mazelle here. *I'd best start packing. I will not need to take all of my things, which will make it easier. I have already received my letter from Mother and Father about the holidays. Everyone is so excited. Maybe we can stop off and see friends on the way.* Princess Arabella sure hopes so. She loves talking with Lizzie and Rumble, the people of the woods. Their little inn is located at the fort in the Kingdom of Elliceton, which is not very far from the academy. It is a safe haven, a neutral zone. There is no conflict in the kingdom, as it is the most peaceful of kingdoms. That is also the location of King Gerald's meetings. Even Lord Hoaggie, the director of the military academy, attends the meetings. The peace and safety of the new worlds is of great concern to all kingdom leaders. The little inn is full of dignitaries every week, trying to solve worldly dilemmas.

With her bags packed, Princess Arabella settles in for the night and drifts off to sleep. All is quiet and peaceful as the princess dreams of family and friends.

CHAPTER 42

The boars are saddled, and all is ready. There is a long line of horses, carriages, boars, elk, and such waiting for their drivers to take them home. The sound of a bell rings out through the building and the grounds, which means the holidays have started. The students stream out of the military academy to their respective rides. All bags are loaded. Prince Elgrin and Hermie mount their boars and wait for the guide to arrive.

"Ah, there he is, Hermie!" exclaims the prince.

"About time, don't you think? It seems like we have been waiting a long time," replies Hermie.

The boys set off for the ride home. The guide has informed them of a mudslide, so they have to take an alternate route. After they have been riding for several hours, they stop to get a bite of lunch and a leg stretch. Lunch is quick. The academy prepared a sandwich, fruit, cheese, and a slice of delicious bumble berry pie—Hermie's absolute favorite—for each member of the party. Hermie is thrilled that there is enough pie for another day.

After lunch, they are ready to continue their journey. It was supposed to be a two-day trip, but because of the mudslide, they may have to travel longer.

They make camp for a long night. Then they are ready for their journey and must not waste any time. There is a chill in the air as they ride. Daylight grows to evening. It will be a much longer trip than predicted. They know they must make camp. The terrain is easier to ride on this trip. They find a little clearing to camp in. Everything is different though. When they came to the academy, the grass was still brown and dull and dreary. Now it is a different cycle. There is cold, white substance on the ground, called "snow," and the air is colder. They set up camp more tightly and closer to the fire. They each have fire heaters for their tents too, which are used for light as well as heat. They are quite cozy.

The travelers are weary from their journey and eat some supper before turning in to their tents. It is a chilly night, and the fire heaters are stoked. Everyone settles in under their blankets for a nice sleep. All is quiet in the camp.

Morning breaks with a terrible howling heard by all.

"What the— What is that?" Prince Elgrin exclaims, bolting up out of a deep sleep. He thinks it sounds like an animal caught in a trap. *Maybe we should check with the guides. They might know what is going on*, he thinks. *I had better see if Hermie is awake. He should be; the howling is awfully loud.*

Hermie emerges from his tent. "What is that howling? Is something hurt?" he asks.

The boys decide to have a quick look before they eat the breakfast the guides are preparing. They sneak off in the direction of the howling but see nothing except a huge albertroken tree not too far from where they have made camp. This isn't just any albertroken tree, though. This tree is special. This tree, to the boy's amazement, has a face on it, and it moves and talks. The stunned pair cannot believe their eyes.

There is a trio of four-legged animals at its base. One is howling as the others make their own eerie sounds. The tree is speaking to them. Having a notion they are being watched, the animals scatter throughout the forest.

Prince Elgrin and Hermie walk toward the huge, ancient tree. Its branches are just settling from the last conversation. The ancient tree begins to slowly sway. "What is it you wish to ask the all-knowing Ernestine? Speak!" commands the tree.

"Who are you?" asks Prince Elgrin.

"My name is Ernestine. I am the tree of wisdom, a wisdom that has been passed down through the centuries by the ancient. Each answer shall be individual, as it comes from a different heart. The answers you seek come from within, as does the question you wish to ask. Go ahead, speak, ask," commands Ernestine. "What is it you wish to know?"

"Well, I have seen a woman in the fog of the Waters of Vision, and I do not know who she is or why I have seen her," confesses Prince Elgrin.

"She was given to you in a vision, a vision only you can decipher. It is buried deep within your memories of youth. Draw upon your strengths and draw your vision out. There are many mysteries attached to the vision. It is up to you to decipher the meaning. Signs come from many places. It may come easily or it may take much deliberation. The answer lies in the stillness of your mind deep within. That is your message. There is nothing more."

The features of the tree slowly disappear within itself, and it looks like any other tree in the forest.

"Prince Elgrin! Hermie! Breakfast!" yells one of the guides.

The two boys run back to the camp, careful not to get into trouble with the guides. They know they will need to sneak away again.

The next part of the journey is a little more harrowing. They must once again brave this new trail around the mountain, and this season cycle makes it more treacherous. The snow on the trails will be dangerous and much harder to navigate. The boars do not have very long legs. It could take even longer to get home in these conditions. The camp sleeps.

It is a brisk morning at the edge of the mountain. Breakfast has been eaten and everyone is loading the boars up. Tents and belongings are packed. The guides are just putting out the last of the fires. Everything is done, and everyone is ready to continue their journey home to Hagville.

The troop starts up the trail to cross the mountain. This will be a long day. After several hours, they stop for a cup of tea and some buzzard jerky.

"Prince Elgrin, come look at the view. It is spectacular!"

"Yes, isn't it the most beautiful scenery you have ever seen? It is lovely with a blanket of snow covering it all. And look way over there. Hagville is almost unrecognizable," the prince replies as he points off in the distance.

With lunch done, they put the fire out and mount up. It is a long journey around the mountain, and with the blanket of snow on the ground, it is more difficult. The troop just carries on. Even at a slow pace, they hope to be back down a hill before dark to make camp. They all know the danger and keep heading down the switchback trails. Boar after boar, step after step, they arduously reach the bottom of the mountain and onto safer traveling ground.

"Finally, we are at the bottom of the mountain. I can't wait to get home. I wonder what feast Mother and Father are planning for my arrival?" comments the prince.

"Oh, I know. I can already taste my mother's water buffalo stew. It just melts in your mouth! I know! I know! Stop talking about food. All we are going to get for supper is gruel unless the cooks at school packed extra," replies a hungry Hermie.

The troop breaks for camp. The tents are hoisted and the fire is started. The guides look for rocks to make a fire ring so the fire will be contained. The two boys help and make a huge fire ring. The fire is burning nicely, and the guides are preparing supper. One of the guides puts a grouse on a spit. Another finds water for tea. *It will be a fine meal*, the hungry boys think as they wait for their supper.

Dinner is ready, and the group eats. With darkness upon them, the two boys tell a few tales by the fire before bedding down for the night. It was much colder today than when they began their journey. They know they must cover up with every available blanket. Everyone snuggles in for a good night's sleep. Tomorrow, barring any trouble, they should be back in Hagville.

The camp is quiet. Until …

The growling noise is so loud that Prince Elgrin jolts awake. He scrambles into some clothes and is outside his tent in a few minutes, only to find Hermie there already. But where are the guides? There is no sign of them. The fire is still hot with embers, so Prince Elgrin quickly puts more wood on the fire, which begins to roar and lift the darkness.

That's when the boys see all the destruction. Three of the five tents are ripped to shreds. There is no sign of the boars or the guides. Neither boy quite knows what has happened. They can't see a track of any sort anywhere. They decide to wait for daybreak before continuing their journey home.

"We have to report this to Father and Mother when we get home. We do not have far to go," Prince Elgrin says.

The boys look around the camp for signs of life or food. They find a few small tins. One contains tea, another a small amount of jerky, and a third gruel. The tins seem to be a guide's secret stash of food. The pair is very glad that the guide was a little greedy. The boys make tea and gruel.

It is a difficult task to go down the mountain on foot. The boys salvage what they can from the camp and packed it up. They try to carry everything on their backs, but it is very tiring. After a couple hours, they stop and build a fire. By the time the water boils for tea, the boys have a new plan. They decide to make a sled on which to carry their gear.

Prince Elgrin drags over a couple of long trees, some large pieces of bark, and small, pliable branches to tie his makeshift sled together. He makes good use of his academy training. His sled looks sound.

Lunch is ready, and Prince Elgrin is very appreciative of the hot tea and gruel Hermie has made for them. The two eat. "You will make a good wife one day." Prince Elgrin laughs.

"Ha-ha. Consider yourself lucky my mother taught me to cook! How is the sled coming along?" asks Hermie.

"I think I have it done. I just need to braid these long pieces of red willow bark and make a rope so we can pull the thing," replies the chilled prince.

The boys finish their tea. Prince Elgrin takes the sled on a test run while Hermie cleans the dishes and puts out the fire. By the time Prince Elgrin comes back, Hermie has packed up and is ready to load the sled. "Ready?"

"Yeah, go on, then. Let's load the sled and hope that it won't fall apart before we get to Hagville," says Prince Elgrin.

With the sled loaded, the boys are ready to continue their journey down the mountain. Prince Elgrin takes the first shift pulling the sled, with Hermie walking behind. Every few hours they switch off.

"Hermie, stop! Come over and look at this!" yells the prince.

Hermie immediately runs around the sled to where the prince is standing. He looks to where the prince is pointing and continues running to a tiny grove of trees. There they are—three of the five wild boars. Now if the boys can only catch them. That will be great.

Hermie returns to the sled. He rummages around in his bag and pulls out a little tin with something in it. Prince Elgrin is puzzled. Hermie shows the prince what is inside this tin: truffles!

"You are a genius, Hermie! When did you get those?" asks the prince.

"Well, we ride wild boars all the time, and this is their favorite treat. I had forgotten that I had some in my bag. So here goes," says Hermie.

He walks ever so slowly toward the wild boars. The boars snort. He stretches out his arm with the handful of truffles. The wild boars' ears are perked and their snouts are high in the air. They smell the truffles. With another snort, they move toward Hermie—slowly at first, then quickening their pace. The closer they get, the faster they run to the smell of the truffles.

Hermie waits for one to get really close. Then he jumps on, grabs its reins, and is off in search for the other ones, which are not hard to find in the snow. Hermie reaches out to a loose boar, who takes a snap at his hand, wanting the truffles inside. Hermie jerks his hand away and quickly grabs the trailing rein. As a reward, Hermie give the newly captured boar a piece of truffle before leading him back to the sled. He does the same with a third wild boar.

With the wild boars back where they should be—one tied to the sled and the boys each riding one—they get back on the trail down the mountain. It is much easier to ride a wild boar than it is to walk, at least for the moment.

A few hours bring them closer to Hagville and farther down the mountain. But in a few more hours, it certainly will be dark, so they must carry on.

The hours pass by too quickly. It seems they have not made much ground. With the switchbacks along the mountain, it is a very long journey home. The boys start to feel hunger pangs. They know they must stop to rest, at least.

Seeing only one more switchback to go, the boys decide to go down it before breaking for a drink and a bite to eat. They know that once they reach the base of the mountain, it will only be hours before they reach Hagville. Hungry and tired, they plod along and finally reach the base of the mountain.

"This is it! Finally, we have made it around the mountain. I can't wait for some hot tea!" exclaims Hermie.

"Me too! Let's get off of these wild boars and give them a break. We need to get something to eat too," suggests Prince Elgrin.

The two dismount and quickly tether the wild boars and make a fire. Hermie puts water on for tea and hands Prince Elgrin some jerky to eat. They do not have much food left and know they will need to get to Hagville as fast as they possibly can. At least at the base of the mountain there is no snow, so traveling will be easier for all.

The boys sit and enjoy their tea and jerky. The light is starting to fade into evening, and they need to be within the kingdom's borders when darkness falls.

"I have kept a keen eye out to see if we have been followed, and I have not seen any trail but ours. My mind is racing to know what happened to the guides, but I cannot think about them now. First we need to get to the kingdom safely," says Prince Elgrin.

"I agree on all counts, Prince. Let's pack up and get a move on. Time is wasting," says Hermie.

The two boys pack up the little they have and snuff out the fire. They mount their wild boars and keep going across the plains. Eventually they enter the huge forest of trees they call home. They are safely on a path now. The journey has become hazardous as they are traveling in the dark, stopping here and there for a small break.

Suddenly they hear *chirp, chirp, chirp*!

"Hermie! Did you hear that?"

"Yes, I did! What is it?"

"I don't know, but it seems so familiar. I just don't know why."

A little blur of bright blue streaks across the lantern light, befuddling the boys.

"I know what that is! I have heard it before, but why can't I remember?" asks the puzzled prince. "Maybe while we are home for these few weeks and have the time, we can investigate on our own and find out what that was."

"Sounds like a plan to me, my friend. Look! Can you see the faint lights of Hagville in the distance? I know they look a lot closer than they are, but we can make it tonight. We can actually sleep in our own beds. What do you think about that?"

"I think it is a fine idea," says Prince Elgrin. He cracks the whip on his wild boar. Hermie does the same. They continue on through the Dreary Forest. The going becomes a little slower again. There are many dead trees and branches on the path they are traveling. They stop here and there to remove debris from the trail.

The pair slowly plod along. Prince Elgrin's hand is getting sore from holding the lantern. Just through a clump of trees, he sees it. He shakes his head just to make sure. Yes! He certainly is seeing it.

"We have made it, Hermie!" yells the excited prince. A few hundred yards ahead of the exhausted pair are the gates leading into Hagville. It was a long journey, but finally they have made it home for the holiday—and sleep. Sleep, a hot meal, and something to drink are all the boys really want. Sleep first, in their own beds, will be enough.

And surely with the news of their arrival and the incidents along the way, the king and queen will be most happy that their son is home safe. Trolby and Edwina will be excited too when Hermie returns to his hovel.

Since it is the middle of the night, the prince and his friend make a pact not to disturb anyone. Prince Elgrin dismounts and opens the huge wooden gates into Hagville. The boys ride through the gates and then close them. Prince Elgrin rides with Hermie to his hovel, bids his friend farewell, and takes Hermie's wild boar along as he rides on to the stable.

The prince puts the wild boars in stalls for the night. It has been an extremely long day, and he just wants to go to bed. He will explain everything about his journey to his parents in the morning.

Prince Elgrin slowly and stealthily makes his way into the castle. He goes quickly to his room. Finally, the boys are fast asleep in their own beds.

CHAPTER 43

"Mazelle! Mazelle! Hurry, we are almost ready to go. The horses are saddled. Come on now, let's get some breakfast and head out. I am so excited to see everyone!" exclaims Princess Arabella.

Captain Mazelle and General Frank emerge from their rooms. Princess Arabella is sitting in the main room, waiting. "Well, it's about time, don't you think? I have been waiting forever for the two of you!" scolds the princess.

Princess Arabella gets off the sofa and leads the trio down to the great hall for breakfast. They eat. A loud bell sounds, and everyone stands. They bow to each other and then to the headmistress's table. Headmistress Vale bows her head in recognition of the gesture. The students file out of the great room and make their way to the foyer, where they don their outer garments. Then they go outside to their rides. This is the cold season of snow.

Francois mans the door, saying his goodbyes to all the students going home for the holidays. Francois laughs robustly at one of his own jokes. With a twinkle in his eye, he smiles at the headmistress. Princess Arabella takes notice and smiles to herself, thinking, *Francois, you sly guy!*

At the front doors, Princess Arabella notices that General Frank is not with Captain Mazelle. "Mazelle, where is General Frank? Isn't he coming with us?" she asks.

"No, I am afraid that General Frank will be staying here for another day to take care of some urgent business. Your father has instructed me to bring you home. General Frank will follow along when his business for the king is finished," replies Captain Mazelle.

"Well, let's go!" yells Princess Arabella, adjusting her scarf. The pair get on their steeds, which are loaded down with luggage and supplies for the trip. They take the trail they were meant to have taken when they came, only to have gotten in a bit of a mess with Norbert. They hope there will not be a repeat of that incident.

It is a long and arduous journey. They stop on a hill and survey their surroundings. Mazelle gets his bearings, and they descend the hill. They will ride as far as the Fort of Elliceton tonight.

It is an uneventful first day. They stop once to rest and water the horses and have lunch. The skies grow darker and darker. The Fort of Elliceton comes into sight. They will be safe within the walls of the fort. Lizzie and Rumble will take good care of their guests.

"It is massive, Mazelle!" exclaims the princess at the sight of the fort.

"Yes, it is. And please, if you may, it is *Captain* Mazelle while we are in the company of others. Is that understood?" snaps Captain Mazelle.

"Yes. I am sorry. When in public, I shall call you by your proper rank, Captain."

"Thank you, Princess Arabella. We are at the gates now."

They wait, looking way up, as the massive gates open for them. The travelers are instructed to take their things to the inn. A servant takes their horses to a stable and makes sure that they have feed, water, and warm blankets. The princess and the captain enter the inn and are greeted by Lizzie and Rumble.

The innkeepers are a sweet pair, really. They wear fringed high boots, fringed jackets, and red sashes around their waists. Lizzie brings out two bowls of soup and instructs her guests to take a seat in the dining room. The pair graciously oblige.

Off one end is a gaming room, where patrons play different games to challenge their wits. Through another door is a staircase to the bedroom suites. Yet a third door leads to the extensive grounds of the fort. It is a very interesting place.

Princess Arabella has heard stories of her father, King Gerald, coming here. The stories always mention the amusements and activities of the king and his friends. Now it is her turn to explore. Princess Arabella thinks that she cannot possibly get into any kind of trouble, because she is inside the fort. Besides that, Captain Mazelle is with her, so what could possibly go wrong?

Princess Arabella and Captain Mazelle are taken upstairs and shown their rooms. They decide to explore before turning in. It is easy for Princess Arabella to lead the poor captain around and get him into trouble. Captain Mazelle is as young at heart as the princess is in age.

Princess Arabella walks across her little room and looks out of the window, studying her surroundings. There are buildings and walkways all over. She does not know what all of the buildings are used for. It is a nice vantage point from here to see everything. She can almost see over the stockade around the fort.

But wait, what does she see sparkling from that building? It looks vacant, but she is not certain. Princess Arabella decides to get Mazelle to go with her. She dashes out of her room.

Knock! *Knock*! *Knock*! "Mazelle! Open up!" yells the princess.

Captain Mazelle's door slowly opens and he peeks out. "What is it now, Princess?"

"Well, it's like this, Mazellie. Either you come with me to explore this place, or I do it alone. Wouldn't want me to get in trouble now, would you?" coos the sly Princess Arabella with a devilish grin on her face.

"Give me a minute to get my boots back on, Princess. Wait there! I will be right out," grumbles Captain Mazelle.

"Okay, I will be right here."

A moment later, Captain Mazelle steps out of his room. Princess Arabella is on a mission. She hurries through the hallway and down the stairs to one of the doors leading to the grounds. The pair sneak outside and creep along one side of the inn. Without being seen, they make their way to the building that the princess noticed from her bedroom.

"Hurry, Mazelle! I think there is someone coming. Get in!" whispers the bold princess. They slink into the building ever so quietly.

"Shh! I think I hear something," says the princess. She slowly creeps to a floor vent on her hands and knees. She motions for Captain Mazelle to come over to her. They look down into a bright room in the basement and see many people at a table. The pair cannot hear what is being discussed. Chairs are moved: the meeting is ending and the inquisitive pair has to hide. All of these people have to leave through the same door the princess and the captain came in. The intruders hide behind some boxes and an old trunk. They are so quiet that one could hardly hear them breathe.

The door on one side of the room opens, and out comes but one gentleman who was in the meeting room downstairs. He shuts the door, scans the area, goes to the outside door, and does the same. He puts on his hood and slithers out of the building.

The princess and the captain wait for more people to exit. There were many people at the meeting. No one comes. Princess Arabella shakes her head and then motions to Captain Mazelle to follow her. Captain Mazelle shakes his head against the move. But she goes anyway, and as the captain is guarding her, he must go with her.

Drat! Silly princess! I wish she would stay in her room until we leave. But nooooo, she has to be an adventurer! thinks Captain Mazelle as he tries to follow the princess.

All is quiet as the pair inch their way down the stairs, seeking the room that was full of people just moments ago. There are many door downstairs. Princess Arabella comes to the door that she thinks may be the one. She reaches out and grabs the doorknob, slowly turning it so as not to make any noise. The door opens a crack. Princess Arabella looks inside and sees nothing. The room is empty. She motions for Captain Mazelle to come in. He walks into the room and shuts the door.

"Well, Mazelle, where did everyone go?" asks the princess in a stern whisper.

Captain Mazelle shrugs and begins looking around. *This is just a meeting room, but where did all the people go who were in here?* he thinks.

Princess Arabella rummages around in a closet. "Mazelle, come look! I found it!" she exclaims.

Captain Mazelle walks over to see what the princess has found. Princess Arabella backs away from the closet and extends her arm so Captain Mazelle can look inside. He sees a hidden door in the floor. He moves a few boxes and opens the door in the floor. He instructs Princess Arabella to find a lantern. It takes a few minutes, but Princess Arabella comes back with a lantern that she has found in one of the rooms.

Captain Mazelle lights the lantern and holds it in the hole in the floor. They see stairs leading down. Just then they hear an unwelcome sound: someone is coming in. Captain Mazelle and Princess Arabella hide in the closet. They wait until the danger has passed.

Once downstairs, they look around in the lantern light. They explore several directions and come upon many doors.

"Mazelle, maybe those people went through one of these doors," guesses the princess.

"Maybe. Let's open one and see where it takes us."

They pick a door and open it slowly, without creaking. They find a long hall. They sneak down the hall, only to find that it leads to a brick wall. They look around, but there is nothing. The captain touches the wall and can feel a little air coming from between the bricks. He investigates further. Sure enough, when he is persistent in pressing on the bricks, a brick door opens just enough for them to peer through.

"Oh, my goodness, Mazelle, where the dickens are we?" asks Princess Arabella.

"I … I … I am not sure, but it looks like a longer tunnel. There are torches on the walls. Should we keep going?"

"Yes, but we need to tie a cloth or string or something so that we are able to find out way back before someone comes to look for us. At least that way we will know where we are. Another five minutes, and then I promise I will go back to the inn quietly."

"Well if you promise, then I will go with you to explore just a little farther. Is that understood, Princess?"

"Yes, just a little farther," mumbles the princess.

The two carry on through the new tunnel. The torches light the way very well. On the left is a stairway, again next to a brick wall, except this time it doesn't look like it will be easy to get out of.

Captain Mazelle tries the bricks to no avail. He looks up the staircase, sees a door at the top, and shakes his head. "I don't think that this is going to happen, Princess Arabella. What if there is someone standing at the door? We can't take the chance that we will be discovered down here. Hurry, let's go back."

Captain Mazelle takes the lead and quietly heads back to the little room on the building's main floor. The two gather their bearings, snuff the lantern, and replace it where the princess found it. Captain Mazelle scouts the outside through a crack in the outer door. All is clear, and Captain Mazelle motions for the princess to follow him.

Finally back at the inn, the two make themselves snug in their rooms and contemplate the adventure they have just been on. Sleep comes easily.

Morning arrives quickly at the Fort of Elliceton. The princess hears people talking and smells breakfast cooking. It really does smell divine. Princess Arabella stirs, wakes, and takes a quick shower. She gets into her traveling clothes and packs her things.

She thinks of the events of the day before and smiles. She wishes she could go down and explore more. She knows that it will not happen and is grateful to have explored the night before, even though she has many questions about the strange events. Why were those people meeting in secret? What was the meeting about? There is too much to think about on the subject. She will talk with Captain Mazelle about it on the way back. It will make the trip go faster.

I think I will have to come back and visit with Lizzie and Rumble. There are many mysteries here, and maybe I could find out about a few of them. I wonder if Mazelle would come and help me find out what secrets lie in that basement, Princess Arabella thinks.

She gives Lizzie and Rumble a hug goodbye. Captain Mazelle is already outside the inn. He has the horses packed and ready. Captain Mazelle is on his steed, and the princess is hoisted onto hers by one of the servants. The pair turn and wave as they ride to the huge entry gates. The gates open, and they continue their journey home.

"What a glorious morning, Mazelle!" exclaims the princess.

"Yes! It certainly is a glorious morning, Princess. Now, no detours. We still have a long journey ahead of us, so please keep up," replies Captain Mazelle. He thinks, *The sooner I get the princess back to the palace, the sooner I can get a break. I hope General Frank will be available to take her back after the holiday.*

Hours pass. "Mazelle, I have to get off this horse and stretch my legs," Princess Arabella demands. She stops and jumps off her horse. She ties her mount to a tree so that it can eat some grass. She begins walking around.

Watching the princess, Captain Mazelle gets off his horse and also stretches his long, thin legs. Then he tends to his horse. Captain Mazelle once again has to caution the princess. "There will be no funny business on the trip back, Princess. The king and General Frank will have my hide if I cannot get you back to the palace safe and sound. Do you understand?"

"Yes, Captain Mazelle, I understand. Let's get a move on! We have a lot of ground to cover." With those words, Princess Arabella rides past the captain and takes the lead. Captain Mazelle, not surprised by her actions, leaps onto his horse and breaks into a gallop to catch up to the energetic princess. They ride at a swift pace for what seems like hours.

Princess Arabella finally slows down and gives her horse a bit of a cooldown before stopping at a little pond on the trail. She lets her horse drink and dismounts. Captain Mazelle arrives and dismounts too. He tethers his horse and lets it drink from the pond. "What is the rush, Princess Arabella?"

"No rush. I just wanted to fast ride for a while. Don't worry. I will keep it slower the rest of the way. I promise," says Princess Arabella and winks. With a giggle, she struts off into the nearby woods for a quick walk to limber up for the next part of her journey.

Captain Mazelle paces as he waits for the princess. It is almost fifteen minutes before she returns. And when she does, she walks right past Mazelle, gets on her horse, and yells, "What are you waiting for, Mazelle? Get a move on!" She giggles and rides off.

Captain Mazelle has Princess Arabella in his range of vision but needs to catch up. He rides at full gallop until he does.

Having crossed the plains, they see the Ruby Forest coming into view. It will take a few hours to reach the trees, but they are making good time. The trail is not too overgrown. After riding for some time, getting closer and closer, the princess says, "Hey, Mazelle! Can you smell that?" With those words, the excited Princess Arabella digs her heels into her horse and gallops even faster.

"Yes, I smell it too—the gardenias. We are close," says Captain Mazelle.

As the princess waits for the captain to reach the Ruby Forest, she watches the brilliant colors of the sunset emerge through the trees of the forest.

Captain Mazelle trots up to the princess. The two gaze at the sunset for a moment and then trot off down the trail. It will be very dark soon; they cover as much ground as possible. Princess Arabella sees that the moon will be full tonight, so they will be able to travel until they reach the palace in Crystal City.

The pair rides for a few more hours. They see a glow in the sky, which means they will soon see the lights of the city. They aren't very far from home.

Finally, they are at the gates of the palace. They ride to the steps of the palace. Princess Arabella jumps off her horse and grabs her gear. She walks into the palace and creeps up to her room to slide quietly into her bed and into dreamland.

Captain Mazelle takes the horses and his gear to the stables. He unloads and settles the horses before he takes himself to his quarters for some rest.

CHAPTER 44

Meanwhile in Hagville, everyone sleeps, but not so peacefully. Prince Elgrin tosses and turns. He shakes his head. Then he yells, "Princess, nooooo!"

The prince wakes in a sweat. He sits up in bed. His special tree-trunk box is on the bed and it is open. There is a flower inside, as fresh as if it were picked today. It startles the prince. He takes the flower out of the box and presses it against his nose. Prince Elgrin takes a deep breath and sighs. He sits for a moment and tries to remember everything from his dream.

"I remember!" I remember!" chants the prince.

Prince Elgrin jumps out of bed after placing the flower back into the tree-trunk box. He runs over to his closet and hides the box. He then gets ready for the day.

Ever so happy to be home, the prince proceeds out of his room and down the hall. The castle is starting to stir after the long night. Prince Elgrin is at the top of the stairs. He climbs onto the railing and slides all the way down, startling Omar and Dee, the two little gossiping rats at the bottom of the stairs. They start chirping away. Prince Elgrin looks at them, winks, and puts his finger to his lips as a signal not to warn the king and queen of his arrival. Omar and Dee let out little squeaks, scoot back to their home under the stairs, and slam their little door.

Prince Elgrin makes his way to the kitchen and bursts through the door. "Goooooood morning, everyone! What a glorious day!"

The startled Queen Hag loses a mouthful of gruel, spitting it all over the king. King Minos looks at the prince, wipes the gruel off his royal attire, and smiles. "Son! When did you arrive? Sit down and tell us all about the journey and school," he says. He hugs his son.

"Son!" squeals the queen as she wipes her face. "You're home!" She runs over and hugs the prince too. "Cook, Prince Elgrin is home! Bring him his favorite breakfast," orders the queen. After several minutes, Cook hurries in with breakfast for the hungry prince.

The three royals catch up on all of their activities of the past few months. It is good for the king and queen to see their son and learn of his adventures at school. Most importantly, they learn that he likes attending the military academy and is head of his class in most subjects.

Hermie pokes his head out of his bedroom door and sees his family having breakfast. There is Hoodly, same as ever, gobbling down his gruel with not so much as a grunt this morning, and then there is Saggerella, who has almost finished her studies to become a pasha. She is talking so much about her studies that she does not notice her little brother walking over to the table. Saggerella suddenly sees Hermie and begins to cough and sputter. She turns red in the face and points. Her worried parents, Trolby and Edwina, turn to see what she is pointing at, and there is Hermie. Edwina drops her spoon and begins to cry. Trolby gives his son a hug. The rest of the family follow, hugging Hermie and excitedly asking him questions about his first term at the military academy, his friends, his classes, his teachers, and more. Hoodly makes room at the table for his little brother. The family has a wonderful breakfast, talking and laughing.

In a few hours, Hermie and Prince Elgrin plan to meet at Soomie Swamp and catch up with each other about their families and what has been going on in the kingdom. So, after breakfast, Prince Elgrin tells the king and queen that he is going to meet Hermie and will be back later. The prince hugs his parents and heads out of the door to the waiting tram.

"Good morning, Prince Elgrin," squeals the little troll at the tram gate.

Prince Elgrin replies and gets into the tram. On the way down, he just can't get the woman in the fog out of his mind. He remembers everything now. But who can he tell? No one besides Hermie—at least not yet.

The tram reaches the bottom, and Prince Elgrin lets himself out. He walks slowly to Soomie Swamp, taking in all the sights and sounds that he has missed all these months. His world is now filled with different sights and sounds—the sounds of the military academy.

There he is, thinks the prince as he sees Hermie waiting at the big rock for him. Prince Elgrin quickens his pace. The boys playfully slap each other on the shoulder. "How was your sleep?" asks Prince Elgrin.

"Great! I have never slept so well. And yours?"

"Hermie, I remember. Do you remember what we saw in the Vision Waters that day?"

"Yes—we saw that girl."

"Do you remember her?"

"What is this about? I don't know what you are trying to say, so spit it out, my friend."

"All right, I will start from the beginning. When I went to sleep last night, I dreamed of her. And when I woke up, I found my special box on the bed. It was open, and inside was a gardenia, as fresh as if it had been picked today. It was all very strange, Hermie, but I remember. I know who she is. Her name is Princess Arabella, and I have to find her. I need to find her," says the lovestruck prince.

"Wow! That is quite a story. Let's put our heads together and try to fit all the pieces of that night together. I don't have the same memories that you do. I was left at the party and don't remember anything else," says Hermie.

The perplexed boys head to their usual shady spot under an old albertroken tree and talk for hours. Finally, at the first signs of sunset and with a plan in hand, they go their separate ways to enthusiastically celebrate homecoming festivities with their families. The tired boys will meet again soon. *The morning will bring many things—including Princess Arabella, I hope*, thinks Prince Elgrin as he walks back to his tram.

CHAPTER 45

*P*eck, peck. Chirp, chirp, chirp. Peck, peck.

"Is that you, Sirus?" asks Princess Arabella upon hearing the sound at the window. The sleepy princess stirs and opens her eyes. As soon as she sees Sirus, she smiles from ear to ear. "Oh, Sirus, I am so happy to see you. I have so much to tell you!" she says as she scrambles out of bed. She goes to the closet and grabs clothes for the day. As she changes, she sees her crystal box on the closet shelf, and it is glowing. *Hmmmm, what is that?* she wonders.

"Sirus, I will meet you outside in about an hour," she says out loud. "I have to go down and say good morning to Mumsy and Father. Oh, yes, and of course have my breakfast, ha-ha."

"Chirp, chirp, chirp!" exclaims Sirus, who then flies right out of the princess's bedroom window.

Princess Arabella goes over to the shelf and picks up her box. Inside the box is a flower, a beautiful purple flower. It smells fresh, and the smell permeates the room. Princess Arabella closes the box and is quite confused. She puts the box back. Still shaking her head, she makes her way to the stairway. It is early, and she hopes everyone is up.

The princess stands at the top of the stairs and looks around from her perch. There are no lights on and no one is stirring. She decides to go outside and see B. L. Rankin, the palace groundskeeper. He will surely be outside.

The princess bounds down the stairs, through the foyer, and out the main doors of the palace. Then she stands on the steps outside, taking in the beautiful colors of sunrise and breathing the fresh, crisp air. She looks around and sees Rankin, as she has called him since she was a child. He is at the stables, bringing out a horse. *I wonder where Rankin is taking it?* she thinks as she runs straight for the stables.

"Hey, Rankin! Wait! Wait!" yells the out-of-breath princess.

Rankin stops and turns when he hears his name. He sees the princess and, smiling, waves at her. "Well, Princess Arabella, when did you arrive home?"

"In the night hours, I am afraid. I have not seen anyone yet. You are the first."

"I am glad. I always love our talks. So how was school and the journey home?"

"Oh, school is all right. The guards are another story, ha-ha. I need to ask you something, Rankin. On the way home, we stopped for the night at the Fort of Elliceton. Lizzie and Rumble were wonderful. What a nice place it was. Have you ever been there?"

"Why, yes, I have, Princess. I have business there every once in a while. Why do you ask?"

"You know a lot of things, and I know you can keep a secret."

"Okay, now you have me intrigued. What is it that you want to know?"

"Well, when we were staying at the inn, I looked out of my window and saw someone sneak into a supply building. The building was small and he never came back out, so ..."

"So ... what did you do, Princess?"

"Well, Mazelle was with me—"

"What did you do? And who is Mazelle?"

"He is Captain Mazelle, and Father had him guard me, along with General Frank."

"General Frank! Isn't he your father's private guard and leader of operations here at the palace? But he was here!" says the confused Rankin.

"General Frank is another story. I will fill you in about him later. I need to tell you this first."

"All right, go on, then. Tell me what happened at the Fort of Elliceton."

"Rankin, we … Mazelle and I … well, we sneaked out of the inn and went to the supply building. We got in and looked through a vent in the floor, and we saw a lot of men around a table. They were having a meeting, but we couldn't hear anything. The men all wore amulets, and there was a symbol on the table, but I couldn't see what exactly it was. A feather maybe?"

"Hmmmmm … a feather, you say?"

"Yes—well, I am not sure, but I think it was a feather. What do you make of it, Rankin?"

"Leave it to me, Princess, and I will see what I can find out for you."

Princess Arabella sees gardeners and servants going here and there. She marches back up the hill and into the palace to have breakfast and see her parents.

Opening the huge entry doors takes a little strength. Princess Arabella knows she can do it. She has been training at school. Once inside, Princess Arabella goes to the kitchen to see Cook. She pushes the door open and yells that she is home and needs breakfast. No sooner has the princess done that than out walk Cook and her mother and father. They are all very happy to see her. The king and queen hug their daughter. Cook gives her a big hug too—after she has set all the food down.

The royal family sit and eat a wonderful breakfast. They laugh and talk for what seems like hours. After breakfast, Princess Arabella tells her parents she is going outside to see her pets. She wants to find Rankin and talk to him some more.

On the grounds, the princess scans to see if she can spot Rankin. There is a lot of action today, and the princess cannot find him. *Oh well, I guess I will just go down to the stables and see if he is there,* thinks the princess.

She hears barking. She turns around to see Monty bounding over to see her. The princess bends to pet him as he jumps up to greet her. In an instant, Monty is on top of the princess, and she is lying on the ground. Princess Arabella laughs as Monty tries to lick her face. "Oh, Monty, I certainly have missed you! And I really could have had you at school with me. I have had a pretty interesting journey, and you probably would have been of some help. Well, except when it came to Norbert!" the princess says with a giggle. Getting up, she dusts herself off and gives Monty another big hug. "Now let's see if we can find Rankin."

Princess Arabella and Monty walk down to the stables. They enter and see a group of stable hands talking. Princess Arabella listens as she walks toward them.

"The king and General Frank's horses need to be saddled and ready right after supper. Makes sure there are a couple of days' worth of provisions with each saddle pack— Princess Arabella!" All conversation stops as the group see the princess. "Wh-what are you doing here? I mean, glad you are home from the academy!" stutters a surprised stable hand as the others scatter.

"I am looking for Rankin. Do you know where I can find him?"

"Yes, Princess. He is in paddock five with a couple of new mares. Would you like one of us to show you where that is?"

"No, I am sure I can find my way, but thank you. By the way, I didn't mean to overhear, but you are saddling a horse for my father. Where are my father and General Frank going?"

"I am sorry, Princess. We just get them ready. We do not question their destination."

"I am sorry. Of course you do not know their destination, and I shouldn't have put you on the spot like that. Carry on, then." She bows, and then she and Monty turn and leave. The stable hands quickly wipe the sweat from their brows. They don't know quite how to tell her where the king is going.

"Only two more paddocks to go, Monty," says Princess Arabella. They have been walking for over an hour. She stops again to scan the area and catch her breath a little. She can see for miles over the rolling hills to a grove of trees on the other side.

The pair continue to walk and play. Monty brings her a stick, and the princess throws it for him. Princess Arabella misses her friend.

Looking to see how far she has walked, she finally sees Rankin with the new mares. They are beautiful and pure white. Princess Arabella walks up slowly with Monty behind her. The mares get skittish, and Rankin looks around. He walks toward the fence. He does not want to get run over by the new herd of frightened mares. Rankin climbs the fence to meet Princess Arabella and Monty. With a huge grin on his face, he says, "Well, hello again, Princess. I was wondering how long it would take you to grace me with your presence again."

"Oh, Rankin, you are so funny! Monty and I thought that we would go for a walk and see the new white mares. They are so beautiful."

"Yes, the mares are quite beautiful. Now tell me why you are really here." Rankin laughs.

"You know me so well. I just wanted to check in to see if you had found anything."

"I have indeed found out a little bit of information for you. The meetings are secret and are attended by members from many kingdoms. These men are entrusted with the huge responsibility of keeping our worlds safe. They are under the leadership of the Kingdom of Likeria. Princess Likeria and your brother, Prince Matthew, oversee the meetings and the security of all of our worlds. What you saw at the inn was the ending of a meeting."

"But who do we need protecting from, Rankin?"

"Well, not all the kingdoms are what we would call friendly. We have to keep the peace and the energy walls strengthened. Our worlds have achieved great peace over the years, and we must keep it that way," replies Rankin.

"Wow! That's a lot. Thank you, Rankin! See you later."

The princess and Monty head over the fence and through the paddocks back to the palace. It is close to suppertime, and the pair is glad to be back. *Maybe, just maybe, I can go to a meeting with Father and see Matthew and Princess Likeria*, thinks Princess Arabella.

She sits on the top step of the palace entrance, places her head in her hands, and ponders what she should do. Monty licks her face. She giggles. Monty always knows how to make her smile.

"Hmmmmm, well, maybe I should follow my father and General Frank," she tells the dog. "Maybe Mazelle will come with me. Maybe not. I will sleep on it." As night falls, the princess goes into the palace, eats her dinner, and goes up to her bedroom.

She sits on her bed and thinks about the events of the day. Then the princess hears a noise outside and wonders what the commotion is. She goes over to her lantern and blows it out. Then she goes to the window and looks out through her curtains. She sees Rankin helping her father onto his horse and General Frank onto his.

Interesting, thinks the princess as she watches the pair ride off into the darkness. *Father never wears the black cloak. I have only seen him wear it when there has been trouble at the wall. Hmmm, why do I have these memories of the energy wall? Perhaps I will investigate in the morning.*

For now, the exhausted princess goes to bed with many thoughts swirling in her head: visions of the gardenia meadow and a boy, a strange boy. He looks different from her. With that fleeting thought, the princess is fast asleep.

CHAPTER 46

The sky is lightening above the trees. *The dull and dreary trees seem strikingly beautiful this morning*, thinks Prince Elgrin. "Well, I guess I should get up and have some breakfast. Hermie will be waiting at Soomie Swamp for me," he says out loud.

He jumps out of bed and gets himself ready. He goes down for breakfast with his family, seated at the huge wooden table.

Saggerella seems to have something on her mind. She fidgets with her spoon as she looks at her little brother. "Hermie, I heard you talking in your sleep last night. You kept calling out a name. It sounded like 'Princess Arabella.' And you kept saying, 'No! No!' Are you all right? Who in the world is Princess Arabella? Is there something that you are not telling us, little brother?"

Everyone begins to laugh and tease Hermie. Of course, Hermie cannot say a word on the subject of Princess Arabella.

Once everyone is finished breakfast, the siblings go their respective ways, clearing out of the house. Their parents, Trolby and Edwina, look at each other with worry on their faces. "Did you hear that, Trolby? Hermie is having the dreams again. Do you think he is talking with Prince Elgrin about it? He must be remembering. We may have to talk to Queen Hag and King Minos again," says a worried Edwina.

"We will leave it for a few days and see what happens. Maybe the boys will just leave the subject alone and get on with things."

"For their sakes, I hope they do. And for the good of the kingdoms."

—m—

Just past the Dreary Forest, through Moogly Marsh, is the home of the Ebbeney Oracle. Inside she sits at a small table. On this table is a piece of cloth. She shakes and drops little bones from her hands onto the cloth. The dimly lit room seems solemn at best. As the lamplight flickers, she reads the bones.

The Ebbeney Oracle gets up and gathers the bones, wrapping them in the cloth. She walks to the door and puts the cloth into her satchel. The Ebbeney Oracle takes her cloak off the hook and puts it on. She grabs her satchel and leaves her home in an ancient albertroken tree to journey to Hagville. There is much going on. The Ebbeney Oracle needs to alert the king and queen of this eclipse that will happen today. Strange things may happen when the earth's energy is momentarily blocked.

She must summon her raven. The Ebbeney Oracle lets out a great caw and waits. There in the distance is Sparaxis. He is coming to his master's call. Sparaxis perches on a branch just above the Ebbeney Oracle, who speaks and lets Sparaxis know of this new development.

The mystical pair starts its journey to Hagville, hoping that they will get there in time, as the eclipse will happen in just a few hours. Enough time is needed to get the prince inside and away from the wall. The draw to go to the energy wall will become extreme.

The Ebbeney Oracle and Sparaxis draw close to Hagville. It is in their sights. In only a few minutes, they will be speaking with the king and the queen of Hagville.

Sparaxis has also alerted Zues and the royal seer of Mystic Mountain. They will work together to keep the children apart and the worlds safe and separate.

The royal pair reach the tram. The Ebbeney Oracle gets into the tram, tugs on the rope, and is hauled up. Sparaxis waits on a rail high above his master.

"We need to keep Prince Elgrin here at the castle. He cannot see her again. If Prince Elgrin were to see or touch the princess, the energy wall would slowly disappear, and the prophecy would come true. The future of the new worlds would be in jeopardy. I hope the prince is still in the castle," the Ebbeney Oracle thinks out loud.

The Ebbeney Oracle reaches the door of the castle. The guard trolls invite the oracle inside. The Ebbeney Oracle is asked to wait and sits in the entryway. Over by the stairs, Omar and Dee are whispering. Upon seeing the oracle, their chatter becomes quick and loud.

"What is *she* doing here?" squeals Dee.

"Don't know, but if she is here, something is going on!"

"Let's go and find Draco. Maybe he knows what is going on."

The pair scuttle under the stairs and slam their door.

The Ebbeney Oracle sits and waits for the troll to come back and take her to the royals. In no time at all, the little troll escorts her to the great room. Minutes are critical. The king and queen are seated on their thrones with vultures on guard.

"King Minos, Queen Hag," affirms the Ebbeney Oracle as she bows before them. The royals reciprocate. "There has been a development. An eclipse will happen today. I know it is little notice, but the bones did not divulge it until today. You must keep the prince inside the castle. The eclipse energies are very strong, and they will pull him back to the energy wall, where he met the princess. We must not let this happen."

"I think our son is in his room. We will have one of the servants check. We will make certain that he stays in the castle for the day," replies Queen Hag. She bellows for a troll to check Prince Elgrin's room.

Another troll escorts the weary oracle out of the castle and to the tram. The Ebbeney Oracle is on her way home.

A little troll whispers something into the queen's ear.

"What! What do you mean, Prince Elgrin is not in his room? Well, don't just stand there! Go and find him! Now! He needs to be in the castle. This is the only place where we can keep him safe. So find him! Gather everyone and find him! Check with Hermie. Go! Now!" orders Queen Hag.

Meanwhile, somewhere by Soomie Swamp, Prince Elgrin and Hermie have already pieced together some of the events from years earlier. The boys remember the energy wall and meeting the golden-haired Princess Arabella.

With his little box in hand, Prince Elgrin and Hermie sneak around Soomie Swamp to the main gates of Hagville. Into the Dreary Forest they go. It is a long journey ahead, and they are prepared. They trudge along, talking.

Prince Elgrin and Hermie stop and sit on an old rotten tree that has fallen. Hermie reaches into his satchel and gets a few snacks for the prince and himself. They are not aware of the chaos happening at the castle.

"Well, that was certainly a great snack, Hermie. But we really should carry on and see what we can find," suggests the prince. They put their things in the satchel and carry on. "It has been many years since we were allowed to come into the Dreary Forest, my friend. It seems even bigger and drearier that it was before." Prince Elgrin laughs.

"Ha-ha. You know that is not possible. It is just because we haven't been here in years—although it really should feel smaller, as we have grown up considerably since then," says Hermie.

"You are right, my friend. It somehow seems bigger, and I really don't know why."

The pair have been walking and talking for a few hours, trying to find something—anything that will lead them back to the energy wall. The details are still a bit fuzzy. They walk and look, and look and walk.

Caw! Caw!

"Shh! You hear that, Hermie? We have to hide. It is one of Mother's vultures flying overhead. We can't be spotted now We are too close to finding the door. That's it! The door! I remember! It is a door we are looking for. We need to find the door to find the energy wall. But hide!" whispers the frantic Prince Elgrin.

Hermie is already under a pile of leaves by a dead tree. Prince Elgrin sees a pile of trees bunched together. He dives to the ground and rolls right under the branches. The boys know that they must not make a sound. The vultures are cunning guards and can hear the slightest movement. The two try not to breathe or make a move.

Hermie has made a bad choice of hiding place. The dust on the leaves tickles his nose until he feels he has to sneeze. He holds his breath and listens.

A vulture lands in a nearby tree, only to find nothing. It swoops off in another direction and then to the castle to report to the king. That is a very good thing, because only seconds after the vulture leaves …

"*Ah-choooooo!*" echoes throughout the forest. With that, there are leaves everywhere. Hermie just sits there laughing, trying to brush leaves off his head and chest. He looks up, and there standing before him is his best friend, laughing and holding his hand out. Hermie hoists himself up with the help of his friend. He brushes the remaining leaves off himself. The pair plods along, still laughing about their close call. But they know that they need to hurry.

It suddenly seems to be getting darker. They quicken their pace. Unknown to them, the eclipse is starting. They keep looking around and walking, hoping to see or find something.

"There! There it is, Hermie! Remember? Remember the door? I think it is over there! Come on!" exclaims Prince Elgrin.

The two run over to what appears to be a door It is even older than they remember, and covered in vines and shrubs, but it is still there. What luck, they have found the hidden magical door.

As the boys walk up to the door, Prince Elgrin reaches into his pocket and pulls out the gardenia that Princess Arabella threw through the energy wall. It still looks as fresh as if it were just picked. Prince Elgrin sees the exact spot where he picked the beautiful purple flower for his special princess. He momentarily is taken back to that time. He smiles and reaches for the handle of the door.

The strong young prince pulls and pulls. The door barely opens. Through the wee crack, Hermie manages to get his fingers into the opening, and he too pulls and pulls. Finally, the great door opens just enough for the two to squeeze through.

The sight is magnificent. Everything is so green and lush. But where is the wonderful sunshine that the boys remember from years before? It seems a little dull and dreary out. What is happening?

The two are too excited to care. They walk and talk and take in the sights. They sit under a huge tree and recall the events of the past.

"Hermie, is it getting darker here? Or am I just not remembering it right? I was sure it was warm and bright and the sun was out as we sat under this same tree," says the prince. Abruptly, he nods off. Hermie cannot even reply, as he too has fallen asleep after their long journey.

CHAPTER 47

Princess Arabella stirs as she hears the familiar *chirp, chirp, peck, peck* at her window. Smiling, she tells Sirus to come in. But this time in fly Ellie and Pooks, her two little wood sprite friends. Princess Arabella is happy to see them. Smiling, she gets up and gets ready for her day, chattering all the while with her little friends. Until this very moment, she did not know how much she has missed them.

With everyone ready and caught up on all the activities of the princess, they decide to go outside. It is very early. As they head for the door, Princess Arabella feels an urge to go instead to her closet and get her flower from her special box. She doesn't know why, but she needs the flower close to her.

Princess Arabella puts the flower into her shirt pocket, and the group leaves her bedroom. They creep out of the palace, ever mindful of the guards. But to the princess's amazement, she does not see any guards. Maybe she will see Rankin at the stables? Standing on the stairs, the princess looks around and does not see anyone. *Hmmmm, I did not think it was that early. No one is even around the stables yet. Oh well, good time for a walk,* thinks Princess Arabella.

Unbeknownst to Princess Arabella, the king and queen have summoned Galena, the royal seer. There have been rumblings in the wind about an eclipse. This eclipse will change their worlds. A magnetic force will try to pull Princess Arabella and Prince Elgrin together. If they have contact, things will change. Worlds will change. It is a good thing that the princess has the little silver ring her brother and his new bride gave her as a gift when they got married. If she gets into trouble, she knows she can count on them.

While Princess Arabella and her little friends are laughing and enjoying the day, Galena arrives at the palace. The hour is still early, and the king and queen must be summoned. Galena is led into a meeting room. She goes over to a small table to set out her crystal ball.

Galena takes off her purple cape and cloaks the table with it. Saying a few magical words, she grabs the cape and flips it off quickly. She then folds the cloak and hangs it on a chair.

Galena softly rubs the crystal ball and chants. She is beginning to see. The smoke in the ball clears. The first thing she sees is the eclipse. Galena gasps. She looks up, only to find that the king and the queen have arrived. *How can I tell them of this?* thinks Galena.

"Good morning, Galena. Why the urgency? What is this about? Is Prince Matthew in danger? We have not seen him or Princess Likeria since the wedding," says the worried Queen Amelia.

"Good morning. I am sorry to alarm you, King Gerald and Queen Amelia, but it is not good. It is also not about the prince and his bride. It is about your daughter, Princess Arabella," states Galena.

"My daughter? Are you sure?" asks King Gerald.

"Yes, I am sorry, but it is about Princess Arabella. Today there will be an eclipse, and it will pull your daughter and Prince Elgrin to the very spot where they had first encountered each other. The pull of the energy wall will be great. The royal pair will not be able to resist it. You will need to protect your daughter. Make sure that she does not see the eclipse and stays in the palace today."

"When will the eclipse happen?"

"The time is near. That is all I know. You must do everything in your power to keep Princess Arabella in the palace during the time of the eclipse. The moon will be very cold and blue, and then a blackness will blanket the world for a few moments. It is during those moments that the prophecy can be fulfilled, so it is imperative that the princess be inside the palace."

"We understand the importance of keeping our daughter in the palace all day. Thank you for coming and alerting us, Galena. We will do what is necessary," says King Gerald. He bows to the royal seer and turns and walks out of the meeting room.

"As always, it is my duty to the kingdom and to you, Queen Amelia. If you need my services during this time, I shall be here." Galena bows in return.

"Goodbye and thank you, Galena my old friend," replies Queen Amelia.

Galena gathers her things. She swiftly leaves the palace.

The princess decides to go to the gardenia meadow. It has been many years since she has been allowed into the Ruby Forest. *Today is the day*, she thinks. *It would be nice to see it, and maybe I will pick flowers for Mother like I used to.*

Princess Arabella and her little troop—which includes the wood sprites, Monty, and Sirus—meander at a slow pace through the grounds and slowly enter the Ruby Forest. "Look at how tall the trees have gotten, Ellie," says Princess Arabella as she looks high in the sky. Light just streams through the tall trees. The princess smiles and keeps walking.

The walk makes the princess a little hungry. She searches her bag and finds a few snacks. She even has snacks for Monty and Sirus. The wood sprites flutter around to find pine nuts. The group sits on the grass and eats.

After their rest, the group continues on their way, jumping over old dead trees and playing little games as they walk. One of the most fun games is spot-the-mushroom—or flower or bird. It is such fun for them all to laugh and reconnect. It has been some time since the princess has seen her friends.

"Shhh!" says the princess. "Do you hear that? I wonder what it is. Shhhh! Let's get a little closer." The princess crouches on all fours and crawls toward the sound. She peers through the underbrush and tries to see what is making such a noise. Surprised by what she sees, the princess lets out a little giggle. "It's a deer with a fawn. I guess that makes sense, as we are nearing Deer Meadow. Ha-ha."

The princess gets up and brushes herself off. With that noise, the deer and fawn are startled and go deeper into the forest. Princess Arabella has forgotten how far away the gardenia field is. They march on.

"Ah, finally! Here we are at Deer Meadow. It won't be long now," she says. "What a wonderful meadow. The sun beaming through the trees makes it just lovely. Is the sun already starting to go down? It is suddenly getting darker. Oh well, we will keep going. Mother would really like some fresh gardenias for her nightstand."

They take a little break and have a few laughs. The wood sprites tease Monty and Sirus, swooping this way and that. *What a fun day with my friends,* thinks Princess Arabella.

"Look there! Is that the gardenia field?" asks Princess Arabella.

It is. The little group breaks into a run to get there.

"Ah! Smell that, everyone! The air is so fragrant. It is no wonder Mother loves gardenias." The princess starts to pick some. She inhales a large breath of the fragrant aroma. "Mmmmm. Just smell that. It is magnificent."

As she picks gardenias, her friends play. She does not notice the growing eclipse. The moon is starting to pass by the sun and cover it. The little troop is unaware of what is really happening around them.

But at the palace, it is another story. The servants have just come from the princess's room; it is empty. Everyone is out searching for her. The king has sent word for Prince Matthew and Princess Likeria. They are the keepers of the worlds and need to know what is happening. He hopes they will make it in time—in time to save Princess Arabella and all the kingdoms of the new worlds.

"We are almost there, Likeria," declares Prince Matthew. The worried couple rides like the wind from the Kingdom of Likeria to the Kingdom of Crystal City.

"It is getting darker, Matthew. We must hurry!" remarks his beautiful wife.

"We are close now. We will stop briefly at the palace and check in with Father, and then we will carry on to the gardenia field. I hope we will be in time to save my little sister," states Prince Matthew.

"We have to be in time, Matthew. If the two meet at the energy wall, all our worlds will be in danger. Things will never be the same!" shouts the distraught Princess Likeria.

At last they reach the palace. Prince Matthew sees Rankin at the stables and decides to check in with him first. Rankin turns and sees the pair riding swiftly toward him. The royal pair's horses come to a screeching halt. Prince Matthew and Princess Likeria dismount. After pleasantries are exchanged, the trio discuss recent events.

Rankin is rather surprised, as he has not yet been informed. Prince Matthew instructs him to saddle up more horses and have them ready for the king, queen, general, and others.

Prince Matthew and Princess Likeria mount their horses and gallop to the palace, where once again they dismount and ascend the stairs to the palace.

After a brief moment inside, Prince Matthew and Princess Likeria are followed out by King Gerald, Queen Amelia, and General Frank. Close behind are Captain Mazelle and the rest of the troops. The royals mount their steeds and are on their way to the gardenia field to rescue Princess Arabella. Rankin bids them a successful journey. He wonders if the princess will be safe and the energy wall intact.

If… Rankin cannot bring himself to think of the alternative. The state of their worlds must remain the same. With the disintegration of the energy wall, pandemonium will ensue. Rankin saunters slowly back to the stables, hoping all will be well with the kingdom.

In Hagville, everyone is frantically trying to find Prince Elgrin and, of course, his best friend Hermie. The Hagvillians are leaving no stone unturned. There are trolls dragging Soomie Swamp. Troops are everywhere looking, and still nothing.

"The Dreary Forest! Get to the Dreary Forest!" screeches the queen.

Trolls and vultures scatter to get to the Dreary Forest.

"Didn't vultures already search the Dreary Forest?" asks King Minos.

"Yes, and they had nothing to report. I have sent them back again. And they will stay there until we find them!" screeches Queen Hag.

"Hoodly! Hoodly!" yells King Minos.

"Yes, King Minos," says Hoodly as he scurries over.

"Get the chariot ready, and be quick about it. I will be down in a few minutes. And saddle up the boars. We will need all of the troll power we can muster to find our Prince Elgrin. Oh, and don't forget to inform Trolby and Edwina! They will want to be there when their son is found!"

"Y-yes, King Minos. I am on it!" stammers Hoodly. He rushes off to the stables to get the wild boars ready. He doesn't have much time.

Prince Elgrin suddenly is shaken awake. He looks up to see Hermie. Hermie is pointing to the energy wall. Prince Elgrin is shocked at what he sees. There is Princess Arabella! She is with a dog and some wood sprites. The princess is picking flowers, just like the very first time they met. He must go and see her and show her the gardenia he has kept all of these years.

With much excitement, Prince Elgrin and Hermie run through the green, green grass to the energy wall. They stop and stare. Prince Elgrin tries to get the princess's attention by waving his arms and yelling. But the princess is oblivious to the commotion.

It is Monty who first alerts her. Princess Arabella stops picking gardenias and turns to her dog. He barks and lunges toward the energy wall. Princess Arabella finally looks up and sees the prince.

The princess is absolutely stunned to see him. He is the boy from her dreams—or were they dreams at all? She is starting to remember. The boy is … Prince Elgrin. He is Prince Elgrin, but not such a boy anymore. The princess smiles.

Princess Arabella remembers. She sets her mother's flowers down and runs to see her friend. She stops as she remembers the flower in her pocket. She pulls it out and holds it in the air to show the prince that she remembers and has kept the flower for years, although it looks like it was just picked.

Then the royal truants hear their parents coming. The thundering of hooves is incredible. It is getting darker and darker as the moon moves in front of the sun, making a powerful eclipse.

The princess has almost reached the energy wall. With all her memories returning, she runs even faster, hoping to see her prince once again.

The darkness is overtaking the day. Prince Elgrin yells to her to throw her flower through the wall. She seems to hear him and throws the flower when she is close.

Their parents are not far behind. They see their children facing each other at the energy wall. They also see the coming eclipse. It is almost becoming impossible to see through the darkness.

The opposing kingdoms riders suddenly fall silent as they watch their children reach for each other, their flowers sailing through the air with poofs of smoke as they cross the energy wall. As the moon eclipses the sun, all is still.

The darkness only lasts a few minutes. The small crowds gathered on each side of the energy wall are paralyzed with fear.

Then Princess Arabella and Prince Elgrin embrace as the energy wall disintegrates around them.

PART THREE

CHAPTER 48

Everything seems to stand still as Prince Elgrin and Princess Arabella embrace. Princess Arabella gazes into the eyes of her prince. She has never felt this way before. She is very much drawn to him. There and then, she knows that he is the one. He is the one she shall marry.

Prince Elgrin cannot move his eyes from her gaze. Princess Arabella is the most beautiful, perfect being he has ever seen. There is an unexplainable connection between the two. Prince Elgrin knows he cannot let her go. She will be his wife.

Within minutes, the trance is broken by both sides yelling and dashing around the two. Prince Elgrin and Princess Arabella are pulled apart with force. King Gerald has the arm of Princess Arabella and Queen Hag has her hands on Prince Elgrin.

Suddenly, a loud chirping and fluttering of feathers is heard. All parties look to the sky and see Sirus the bluebird. He lands on the ground in front of the prince and princess. Sirus begins to transform into the shape of a woman. She is tall, with long, white, straight hair. Mixed in are strands the colors of the rainbow. She wears a crown of vines interwoven with crystals upon her head. She is clothed in a long cloak of blue velvet with long sleeves and a crystal-and-vine belt. Her cloak is of matching color. Even her eyes are the same deep blue. They seem to sparkle somehow. She has a staff in hand.

"Who are you? What are you? What is happening? The prophecy is true!" yell the crowds gathered at each side of the energy wall.

The being who was Sirus holds up both hands and motions for silence. The crowds quiet as she begins to speak.

"Do not be afraid! I am the Kalliac. I come from a place beyond time and space. It is named Sirus. I have been sent here to help you with the integration of all kingdoms. I have been sent because of the prophecy—the prophecy of the new world. I have come to protect the chosen ones. They are the ones who shall carry the kingdoms to the future, into the new world. The chosen ones will bear the heir to all kingdoms so that the world shall continue. The integration will not be swift. It will be troublesome, and some concessions will have to be made. It will be the way into the new world. The new world is a world of peace, a world of compassion, and a world of joy. There shall be no wars. There shall be compromise. There shall be love. There shall be empathy toward your fellow man. There shall reign peace and harmony upon all the lands. I am the Kalliac! I am an Ancient One!"

"The energy wall is gone! Great Kalliac, what do we do now? Kingdoms that were once protected from harm lie open to predators and ruin. How do we integrate with the likes of the Loki, the world troublemakers, and the Kingdom of Amari? All kingdoms are not peaceful like ours. We have spent many moons trying to protect our kingdoms from such harmful and destructive ones. And what now? Integrate? Welcome such forces into the peacefulness of our own kingdoms? It surely cannot be done!" retorts King Gerald.

"And what is this about chosen ones? They are from different kingdoms, of different colors. How are they to bear an heir to the future when they do not belong to one kingdom? They shall bear a mixed blood? What is that? How do we deal with that? Is that even possible? That cannot happen, great Kalliac, it just cannot happen!" blurts out an angry Queen Hag.

King Minos helps to steady her, as she is visibly shaking and very upset. Everyone is at this moment. Everyone is shaken to their core. How can this be? How? No one can comprehend the consequences of the destruction of the energy wall. What chaos will be brought into their kingdoms?

Kalliac throws her arms above her head. A great crack is heard in the sky. Everyone settles down as she speaks again.

"King Gerald, I am requesting that you and your kingdom welcome all heads of state from each kingdom for a grand gala—a gala that I shall attend. I shall help to calm your fears and mediate any concerns the kingdoms have as we enter into the new world." With these words, the great Kalliac is transformed back into Sirus, the little bluebird.

No one can believe what has just happened. They are all stunned. Has this been the grand plan from the very beginning? Sirus only showed up after the birth of Arabella, the last child born in the Kingdom of Crystal City. Did the prophecy begin before that? There are so many questions going through the minds of everyone.

King Gerald pulls his daughter to him and hugs her. He hesitates, then steps aside to face Prince Elgrin and extend his hand. Prince Elgrin graciously shakes it and introduces himself as Prince Elgrin from the Kingdom of Hagville. The prince introduces his parents, Queen Hag and King Minos. They all nod in kind. King Gerald then introduces his family. He lets King Minos and Queen Hag know that he will make arrangements for the grand gala. All nod in approval and retreat from the energy wall.

No one is in a hurry to leave. They are all in awe at the happenings of the afternoon. They slowly walk home in silence.

CHAPTER 49

At the vine-covered door. Prince Elgrin pushes it open with great ease. It swings open. *Strange,* thinks the prince. *It is the prophecy! It opens with great ease now as the energy wall is no longer.* Shaking his head, he holds the door open for his mother and father.

The royals walk in silence. The guards march slowly behind. Prince Elgrin and King Minos help the distraught Queen Hag maneuver over fallen trees. After much walking, they finally see the guard standing at attention at the royal carriage. The guard helps the queen and the king board the old, rickety carriage. Prince Elgrin swiftly jumps in and takes a seat on the dusty old cushions. The guard cracks his whip, the boars let out a frightful squeal, and the carriage moves with a jerk. It cracks and grunts through the Dreary Forest, along the old trail to the gates of Hagville.

The carriage pulls up to the tram. The guards help Queen Hag step out of the carriage, followed by King Minos and Prince Elgrin. The guards take the carriage to the stables while the three royals proceed to the tram. They are awaited by the little green-haired troll guard, who hauls them up. One by one the royals are lifted to their treetop castle. the little troll grunting and groaning with every pull of the rope.

Prince Elgrin is the last one to arrive. He walks to his parents, and they continue on to the castle. It is a silent walk. They reach the castle doors, and two trolls open them. The royals enter the castle.

Two little rats watch from their perch under the stairs. The royals are quiet as they go into the royal kitchen.

"Omar! Did you see that? No one was speaking! There is something going on!" squeals a puzzled Dee.

"Yes! Yes! There is something going on! Something big! And we are just the rats to find out what! Yes, indeed, we will find out what!" squeaks Omar.

The two fat little rats scurry into the doorway of their home at the bottom of the stairs and slam the door.

The castle is already buzzing that something is desperately wrong, and no one has said a word yet. Tension fills the air. The staff all look worried as the royals take their chairs at the kitchen table.

"Cook!" screams Queen Hag.

"Yes, I am here, my queen," replies a startled Cook.

"Would you bring us tea and light snack, if you would," asks King Minos.

"Yes, right away, King Minos," says Cook. She scuttles away into the kitchen.

Within minutes the silent royals are given tea and food. They consume their tea and snack in silence. Finally, King Minos speaks. "Elgrin, my son, I have no words at this time as to the situation that faces us all. There has been great pressure put on you alone by the Ancient Ones. With the disintegration of the energy wall, there is much to consider. The consequences are enormous. Expecting the kingdoms to integrate peacefully is unimaginable. I just don't know how we will accomplish this great task—but we must try, for the good of our world. With that said, we will retire to our rooms and meet in the morning to decide what we will do next."

The queen and king stand. They hug their son and leave the room.

Prince Elgrin feels overwhelmed by the happenings of the day. His only thoughts lie with the beautiful Princess Arabella: her long mane of golden hair, the crystal blue of her eyes, and the beauty of her smile. Finally he has held her, after all this time. From their very first meeting, he knew that there was something special about her. He is destined to be with her.

Prince Elgrin stands, takes a deep breath, and leaves the kitchen. It has been a long day, and prince goes up to his room for some needed rest and contemplation.

CHAPTER 50

King Gerald exchanges a worried look with his wife, Queen Amelia. King Gerald has her arm as they walk to their horses in the gardenia field. Prince Matthew and Princess Likeria have the arms of Princess Arabella, who is in shock. She cannot believe what happened to Sirus. The little bluebird is actually an Ancient One. Her little friend, whom she has known her whole life, is not who she thought he was. She has been watched over this whole time for her destiny: to play her part in the beginning of the new world.

The royals are sheltered by guards as they mount their horses and begin the ride back to Crystal City. It is a slow ride through the gardenia field. Entering the forest, they see deer watching them as they ride. Soon they are in Deer Meadow. The sun's rays beam into the meadow, making Princess Arabella smile. The ride continues in silence out of the forest. In the distance, the palace in Crystal City can be seen.

Princess Arabella suddenly lunges ahead of the group and gallops like the wind to the palace grounds. Rankin is standing at the doorway of the stables. The princess gallops over to him and dismounts. Rankin takes the horse from Princess Arabella and leads it into the stables. He removes its saddle and shuts it into a stall, all the while noticing how forlorn the princess seems. "What seems to be the trouble, Princess Arabella?" he asks.

"Oh, Rankin, you will never believe what has happened! The energy wall is gone and I have met Prince Elgrin of Hagville and Sirus isn't a little bluebird and she is an Ancient One and—"

"Whoa! Slow down, young lady. I can't make out a thing you say. Start from the beginning."

"Well, I went to the gardenia field to pick some flowers for Mother. While I was there, Monty was going crazy. I turned around and saw a boy on the other side of the energy wall. I had seen him before on my birthday, many years ago. So I went over to the wall, and we talked. Then we noticed that our parents were coming toward us on either side. We threw our flowers through the energy wall and moved in to touch hands, because we thought we might never see each other again.

"Then it got dark. I stumbled and landed in the prince's arms. That was where I was when the sun came back. Our parents and guards were standing at either side of us. The energy wall was gone! They were reaching for us when Sirus came out of the sky, wildly chirping. He landed on the ground in front of us."

She is interrupted in her story as the rest of the horses and riders reach the stables. The riders dismount and bring their horses in. Rankin gives Princess Arabella a nod, and she knows that their conversation is over for now. She will catch up with him later and finish telling her story.

Princess Arabella runs to catch up to the other royals returning to the palace. She meets them going up the stairs. The guards open the doors for the royals. Prince Matthew and Queen Amelia are followed in by Princess Arabella and Princess Likeria. Once the queen and princesses are settled with some tea in the sitting room, Prince Matthew heads back outside to consult with his father, King Gerald.

At the stables, Prince Matthew sees his father talking with the guards and B. L. Rankin. The guards are gathering fresh horses. Prince Matthew approaches the king and B. L. Rankin.

"What's going on, Father?" asks Prince Matthew.

"I am going to rally some of the kingdom leaders to discuss what has just happened. I want you to stay with your mother and sister and wife. I also want you to coordinate security measures with the unicorn captain to continue to protect the kingdom. We will meet again when I get back."

Matthew nods and heads back to the palace. He directs the staff to get accommodations ready for Princess Likeria and himself. The right wing of the palace will be theirs.

Prince Matthew goes to the sitting room, where his mother and wife are still having tea. "Is your father not with you?" asks Queen Amelia.

"No, Mother. Father is at the stables, getting ready to meet with other kingdom leaders to discuss what has gone on with the energy wall. I came to check on the all of you. Father wants you to be safe," says Prince Matthew. "Princess Likeria, the staff has prepared a suite for us to use for the next few days. After that, we will need to go back to the Kingdom of Likeria and see that things are good there. Please rest, and I shall see you in a few hours, my dear." He kisses his wife.

Prince Matthew goes back to the stables and sees that his father is already gone with some of the guards. Captain Mazelle and General Frank remain to guard the queen and princesses. Prince Matthew saddles his horse and heads to the energy wall to meet with the captain of the unicorn guards. He rides swiftly, but it is a long ride. Travel is a little slower through the forest but the prince still makes good time.

The smell of gardenias is incredible. Prince Matthew is close. In the distance, he sees the unicorn captain and rides to meet him. The unicorn guards are still vigilantly patrolling the border where the energy wall used to stand. Now there is nothing but an imaginary border.

After he has reviewed everything with the unicorn captain, the prince makes his way home to the palace for much- needed food and rest. At nightfall, the prince checks on the queen and Princess Arabella. Both are settled into their rooms for the night. There are guards at each door. The prince goes to his own quarters, where Princess Likeria waits. All is quiet at the palace.

Meanwhile the king is almost at his destination: the Fort of Elliceton, in the valley where two rivers meet. Kingdom heads have been alerted and will meet the king within the hour. This emergency meeting is needed to make a transition easier for them to handle. Having no energy wall is quite a problem, one that requires serious discussion. How will they protect themselves and integrate with other kingdoms? It is a dire situation that he hopes will slowly resolve itself.

In the distance, he sees lights—the lights of the fort. The king and his guards quicken their pace. They ride up to the gate and rap on it. The gate opens, and they ride to the stable at the inn. The gate closes behind them. They dismount and go into their secret meeting room.

Lizzie has everything ready, even food and drink set out for the weary travelers. The king and his guards enjoy it while waiting for others to arrive. One by one, with their guards, the rest of the kings arrive. Everyone takes their positions at the table, and the meeting begins.

There are thirteen kings present to discuss events. The meeting is called to order. The first item of discussion is what happened in the Kingdom of Crystal City. Then, one by one, the leaders speak of what happened in their kingdoms as the energy wall fell. Hours pass. When all the kingdoms have spoken, King Gerald tells them about the Kalliac, the Ancient One. Kingdom leaders do not know what to think about this Kalliac, but they understand that they need to discuss the possibilities of this new world, a world of integration and peace.

"Apparently the Kalliac has been here for many years, watching and waiting for the day the energy wall would fail. She has been here to watch over the chosen ones, one of whom is my own daughter,

Princess Arabella. The other chosen one is Prince Elgrin of Hagville. Much to my dismay, the two of them will start a new world. When a child is born of the two, the integration will be well on the way to beginning a new kingdom, an integrated kingdom and a new world. The Kalliac will keep them safe. In making this new world, we need to keep ourselves and our kingdoms safe as well. We know full well the Loki and Amari live to fight. They live for war, even among themselves. So, gentlemen, any ideas as to where we go from here?" asks King Gerald.

"It is of my opinion that borders still need to be enforced for each kingdom. We need to have some kind of control of our own people. We will have to establish identification for members of our communities. When they wish to cross a border, we can document them and know who is in our kingdoms. We can come together in healing practices and learn new techniques. It could be beneficial for all of us, especially in a peaceful environment. We really have no choice but to try," says King Taras of the Kingdom of Ghost Valley.

"All good and welcome ideas. We will talk about them at length later. But there is one more thing I have come to discuss. The Kalliac asked the Kingdom of Crystal City to hold a special gala for all the kingdom leaders, along with The Kalliac, to make introductions and exchange information. Gentlemen, I motion for the gala to be held in three weeks. That will give everyone enough time to travel to Crystal City for the gala. Invitations will be sent out in the morning. Now let's get back to business," states King Gerald.

The talks go on for much of the night. Daybreak nears before the talks conclude. The kings rise and, with salutations, slowly file from the room. The last to leave is King Gerald.

CHAPTER 51

It is morning in the Kingdom of Hagville, and the queen is awake. She looks around their quarters for her husband, King Minos. He is not there. Queen Hag leaves their quarters. She walks the long hall and down the huge staircase to the kitchen. The king does not seem to be there either. Queen Hag sits down and shouts, "Cook!"

"Yes, my queen," says Cook as she enters the dining area.

"Has King Minos been in this morning? And what about Prince Elgrin?"

"Not yet, your highness."

"Bring me my breakfast!" says the queen.

"Yes, my queen," says Cook. She hurries back into the kitchen to prepare the queen's breakfast.

Minutes later, Prince Elgrin arrives in the kitchen, seeking his breakfast. "Good morning, Mother. Did you sleep well?" he asks as he kisses her on the cheek. He then goes to his place at the table and takes a seat.

"Yes, I slept extremely well—in fact, so soundly that I did not even hear your father rise and leave the room. Have you seen him this morning?"

"No, I have not, but I am sure he will soon be here for his breakfast."

Cook enters the dining area with the queen's breakfast. She nods at Prince Elgrin and goes back to the stove to prepare his breakfast.

The queen eats in silence, thinking about what might have happened to the king. Then the door to the dining area opens, and there stands King Minos with his cloak on.

"Minos, where have you been? I have looked all over the castle for you!" says a worried Queen Hag.

"There was a meeting," replies a very tired King Minos.

"What do you mean, a meeting? You could not inform me of such a meeting?" retorts the queen.

"No. You were sound asleep when the scroll arrived. So I left you to sleep," says the king. He removes his cloak, drapes it on a chair, and sits down.

Cook, hearing the king's voice, brings in breakfast for the prince and king. She sets a tray of food on the table, hands out individual plates, and disappears back into the kitchen. The royals enjoy their breakfast before engaging in more conversation.

"We have much to do in the coming weeks, my queen. We will be attending the gala at Crystal City. We have many arrangements and changes to see to within the kingdom. The first of many will be to patrol the border where the energy wall used to be. We must assign guards. We must also establish some form of identification for our people. There is much to do if we are to be part of this new world. We have not been given a choice in the matter, so we must comply. The Kalliac will want to see progress; I am sure of it. But for now, I need a little rest. Prince Elgrin, will you see to it that guards patrol the border where the energy wall used to be?"

King Minos turns to leave the dining area and go to his quarters for much-needed rest.

"Father, wait. May I walk with you? I need to discuss something with you."

"Yes, my son. What is it?"

"Well ..." The prince hesitates. "I would like to see Princess Arabella, if I have your permission."

"Yes. Apparently you are a chosen one. We do not really have a choice. Ask your mother to send word to Crystal City for you to meet with the princess. I want you to meet close to the border with your guards. Maybe in the gardenia field—it is close to the border, and you will be safe there. Is that understood?"

"Yes, Father," says the excited Prince Elgrin. He bounds back to the dining area, where his mother still sits contemplating all that has happened.

"Mother, Mother, Father has given me permission to see Princess Arabella! He wants you to send word to Crystal City. He wants me to meet her at the gardenia field close to our border. I will have guards with me as well. P-p-please, Mother," stutters the prince as he pleads his case.

"I guess we have no choice in the matter, since you are a chosen one. Best get to know your future bride," mutters the queen.

Queen Hag leaves the kitchen and makes her way to the sitting room to write an invitation to Princess Arabella. She gives the scroll to a vulture to deliver to Crystal City. One scroll done and one to go: the Ebbeney Oracle is next. Queen Hag scribes another scroll. Another vulture is summoned and given that scroll. The queen waits for replies.

Now for some tea, she thinks, and calls for the servants to bring her tea and stoke the fire in the sitting room. The queen enjoys the peaceful moments she has while waiting. Once King Minos wakes, there will be much to discuss and plan for, with the future of the kingdom at stake. All is momentarily quiet in the castle.

CHAPTER 52

Everyone is up and ready for the day at Crystal City. The royals are all downstairs and seated at the kitchen table, awaiting breakfast, except the king. Within minutes the king also arrives for his much-needed breakfast. Pleasantries are exchanged across the table and breakfast is served. The hungry royals dive in and enjoy their breakfast.

"How was the meeting?" asks Queen Amelia.

"Well, many things were discussed, and I think we have come to some resolutions regarding the energy wall and the chosen ones," says the king as he glances at his daughter, Princess Arabella. "We have much to do. Prince Matthew, can you check in with the unicorn guards and see about the status of the border? Amelia would you request the presence of Galena, the royal seer? We should speak with her. Also, here is a list of the kingdoms to which we need to send invitations for the gala. Please get this to the royal scribes. The gala shall take place in three weeks. We must establish some form of identification for our people as well. Princess Likeria and Princess Arabella, if you would help the queen with the invitations, I would much appreciate it. With that said, I must get some sleep. The night was very long. I will check in with you all in a few hours," says the exhausted King Gerald. He gets up and starts to leave the dining room.

Suddenly a loud squawking is heard at the window. Perched on the windowsill is a vulture holding a scroll. King Gerald walks to the window and takes the scroll from the vulture's beak. The vulture waits. King Gerald breaks the seal and reads the royal scroll. He sits down.

"What is it?" ask Queen Amelia and Princess Arabella in unison, looking at the king.

"It is an invitation for Princess Arabella. Prince Elgrin requests your presence. He wants you to meet him at the gardenia field for a picnic to get to know each other. In the company of guards, of course, and near the border for safety. 'If it suits you to attend, send a reply with the vulture. Graciously signed, Prince Elgrin.'" King Gerald looks at his daughter, who is beaming. Prince Elgrin has not left her thoughts since she saw him the day before.

"Oh, please, Father! I would really like to get to know him. I cannot get thoughts of the prince from my mind. If indeed we are the chosen ones, then we should know each other. We need to see if it is truth. Please!" begs the princess.

"Oh, all right, I agree with you, princess; you need to know if this is truth. You may reply to the invitation. You may go this afternoon if it suits you," says the king.

"Thank you, thank you, Father!" replies the excited princess. She writes her reply on the scroll, puts the royal seal on it, and gives it to the vulture to deliver back to the Kingdom of Hagville.

CHAPTER 53

Prince Elgrin nervously paces back and forth in the massive great room, waiting for the vulture to return with a reply from Princess Arabella. He hopes she will agree to a meeting at the gardenia field. He holds in his hand the gardenia that Princess Arabella threw through the energy wall. He lifts it to his nose and smells the lovely fragrance that reminds him of the beautiful princess.

A loud *caw* startles the prince. He looks up and sees a vulture at the window with a scroll in his large beak. Prince Elgrin runs to the window and takes the scroll. The vulture leaves. Prince Elgrin sees the royal seal from Crystal City on the scroll and breaks it. There is a reply from the princess. She wants to meet with him! Prince Elgrin is elated. He has never been so happy.

First he must tell Cook to prepare his favorites foods and put them in a basket for him to enjoy with Princess Arabella. With that done, he can go see his friend Hermie and let him know the good news. The excited prince goes into the foyer, and the little troll guards open the massive wooden doors for him.

The two fat little rats are under the chairs, watching and waiting to learn some information. They are completely perplexed as to the goings-on.

"Did you hear that, Omar? What in the world is going on? Is it really true that the prince is going to meet the princess from Crystal City? I just can't believe my ears. You better go through the tunnels and see what you can find out in the kitchen. Oh, and bring us a crumb or two while you are there," suggests a hungry Dee. The two rats scamper to their door under the stairs, enter, and slam the door behind them.

The gigantic doors shut behind the prince. Prince Elgrin looks outside and takes a deep breath.

"What a glorious day! The clouds are low and the forest is dreary. What a wonderful day!" exclaims the prince.

Prince Elgrin walks along many walkways to get to the hovel of his friend Hermie. He passes shops, waving and saying hello to many shopkeepers. Hermie's hovel comes into view. Sitting beside it is Vincent, Hermie's pet rat. Vincent sees the prince and scampers over to him. Prince Elgrin bends down and picks up Vincent. He reaches into his pocket and gives Vincent a nice big peanut. Vincent grabs the peanut. The prince sets Vincent on the ground. The rat scampers away with the nut in his mouth.

Prince Elgrin steps up to his friend's door and knocks several times. He stands waiting for it to be answered. The door opens and there is Hermie. With a smile on his face, Hermie grabs and hugs his friend. Prince Elgrin motions for Hermie to come out for a walk. The two decide to go to their favorite spot to catch up, Soomie Swamp.

They walk over to the tram and one by one step into it. The tram is lowered by little troll guards making the usual grunting and screeching sounds. Prince Elgrin wonders how Princess Arabella will react to his home; she lives in quite a different world. Time will soon tell.

The two friends reach the ground and race to Soomie Swamp. They screech to a halt when they reach their spot: a huge, flat rock, on which they both sit.

"Well, don't keep me in suspense any longer, Prince. No one has said a thing. What went on yesterday? Did you see the princess?" asks an anxious Hermie.

"Not only did I see her, I hugged her!"

"What! How did that happen?"

"Well, I went to the wall and the princess was there. She came over and we talked. Then we threw our flowers through the energy wall. Just as that happened, the sky grew dark—so dark, in fact, that I could not see. All of a sudden, the princess was in my arms. I don't know how it happened.

"Hermie, I am going to make her my bride.

"Of course, our parents were around us on both sides and tried to pull us away from each other. Oh, and then! You won't believe this! The little bluebird that has been helping us landed in front of us and turned into a person. Well, I tell you, everyone was in shock. She was tall and had long white hair with colors in it. She called herself The Kalliac. Apparently I am a chosen one, as well as Princess Arabella. The energy wall is gone. We are all supposed to integrate with each other to make one world filled with peace. Get that! I don't know how that will be done, but that is what happened.

"I am going to see the princess this afternoon to try to get to know her and see if this means anything. It all is a lot to understand. What do you think?" asks the prince.

Hermie is in awe. He doesn't know what to think of what the prince has said. He sits for a few minutes before he speaks. "Prince, I am having a hard time believing this tale. No energy wall? Our little bluebird turning into a person? You and this princess as chosen ones? All kingdoms getting along peacefully? It is like a dream somehow. I just don't know what to think right now. To be free to go to other kingdoms in peace …" says an overwhelmed Hermie.

"Let's go back and I will leave you to think about this. I have to get ready for my meeting with Princess Arabella," replies the prince.

The two friends walk and talk about other things. The mood has certainly changed between the two. At the tram, Hermie says goodbye to his friend and gets hauled up. He doesn't wait for the prince to be hauled up; he goes to his hovel. Prince Elgrin turns the opposite way and walks down the many walkways to the castle, wondering what the princess will think of his kingdom.

Prince Elgrin keeps walking until he reaches the castle. Two troll guards stand at attention at the doors. They hurry to open them for the prince. The prince enters and proceeds straight to the kitchen to check in with Cook about his picnic.

"Did you see that, Omar? The prince is going to check on his food for the princess. It cannot be. Meeting the princess from Crystal City! What is going to happen to our kingdom?" squeaks a worried Dee.

"I guess we shall see. We need to keep our eyes and ears open to find out more. Let's go. I brought back plenty of crumbs for us."

The two little rats scurry to their door under the stairs, go in, and slam the door behind them.

With his basket ready, Prince Elgrin and his guards leave the castle and set forth to the gardenia field to meet Princess Arabella. The prince is very excited to be on this journey today. It is a new day! He absolutely cannot believe what is happening or what has happened. It is just the beginning with no energy wall. Hopeful that all the changes will be good, he keeps his pace with the guards, one in front and one behind. King Minos is not going to take any chances with his son's well-being.

The three trudge on, getting closer and closer to the vine-covered door. With the door in sight, Prince Elgrin has a strange fluttering in his stomach. He can't wait to see his princess. The three walk through the door and straight to the gardenia field, ever mindful of staying on their side of the border until they see the princess. There they wait.

CHAPTER 54

Princess Arabella has chosen to wear some of her finest riding gear, as she will ride this day to see her prince. She wears a crown of vines and flowers in her hair. Ellie and Pooks, the little wood sprites, are going with her to make sure she is okay. Princess Arabella grabs her riding jacket and leaves her room. She looks radiant as she bounds down the stairs and walks straight for the kitchen.

Cook has made her favorite boysenberry tarts for the special occasion. Cook places them in a small basket with some mulberry juice. Princess Arabella thanks Cook with a quick hug and is on her way to meet Prince Elgrin.

The princess is almost at the doors when she hears a stern voice: "Aren't you forgetting something?"

Princess Arabella turns to see Captain Mazelle standing alongside General Frank. "Really? Surely not today! Why can't I go with Ellie and Pooks? The unicorn guards on patrol at the border should be enough protection for me, are they not?"

"Sorry, Princess Arabella, but we have our orders from your father. You are in no way to go on this journey to the gardenia field alone, without protection of your guards. Let's not dally. The horses are saddled and ready. Shall we?" says General Frank. He holds his hand out to the doorway for the princess to lead the way.

Princess Arabella hands her basket to Captain Mazelle and stomps out of the palace to her waiting horse. Rankin helps the princess mount. Horses and riders gallop away through the palace grounds. The general leads the way with the princess in between the two guards.

It seems to take forever to get to the forest. From there, the ride goes a little faster. Princess Arabella talks and giggles with the wood sprites for the whole ride. Ellie flies off, darting here and there. Passing through Deer Meadow, the trio continue in the bright sunshine. There is only the last bit of forest to go through, and they will be there.

The smell alerts them that they are close. As they ride, she sees the prince and his guards just over the border. She breaks from the group and rides as fast as her horse can take her.

Princess Arabella comes to a screeching halt and jumps from her horse. She runs over the border to the smiling Prince Elgrin. The pair embrace. They are happy and overwhelmed to see each other.

Princess Arabella takes the prince by his hand and leads him back over the border to a blanket on the ground, spread out by her two guards. There is a basket sitting on the blanket. The prince and princess sit on the blanket. Prince Elgrin motions for his guards to bring his basket. All the guards back off and surround them from several yards away.

The guards see the baskets being opened and the food being put out. The prince and princess talk and laugh for hours.

General Frank clears his throat really loudly and causes the princess to take notice. Princess Arabella nods, and with a few words to Prince Elgrin, the royal pair begin to clean up their picnic. They grab the baskets and fold up the blanket. Princess Arabella gives the blanket and her basket to Captain Mazelle. Then she walks with Prince Elgrin and his guards across the border. The pair embrace and make plans to see each other in a couple of days.

Princess Arabella watches as Prince Elgrin and his guards walk through the vine-covered door. She turns and walks back across the border with a smile so big she seems to want to burst. General Frank helps her onto her horse. The three begin their journey back to the palace with General Frank in the lead. Again the princess whispers and giggles with the wood sprites. The princess has never seemed so happy.

As they cross Deer Meadow, General Frank puts his hand up, and the trio of riders stop. Standing in the distance is a man dressed very unusually. He wears long, light, brown robes. One lies across his shoulder and attaches at his hip. The material is a very loose and flowy; it looks like some sort of linen. He wears a strange big-rimmed pointed hat as well. His hair is long, and he walks with a staff. Little puffs of smoke come from his feet.

General Frank is stunned. Never has there been another person in Deer Meadow except Crystal City royalty and their guards. With the energy wall gone, things are truly beginning to change.

General Frank rides toward the stranger. He must assess the level of danger before the princess can continue. Princess Arabella stays with Captain Mazelle, and they wait.

General Frank sees that the stranger is standing on what looks like charred earth. He hears, *"Aaa-chooo!"* and flames seem to shoot out from the stranger's side. Then out peers a lime-green face with a long, pointy nose—the face of a strange creature.

The creature slowly steps out. It has four legs and a long tail. It has spikes all over its body and a pair of small wings on its back. It stands only a foot high and is two feet long. It looks like a tiny dragon of legend. General Frank has only heard tales of such things in books. How can this be? What is going on? What is happening? General Frank is so stunned that he can hardly speak to the stranger, but he does. "Who are you, stranger? Why are you on the lands of Crystal City? And what is that animal you bring?" barks the general.

"It would appear that I am lost. I am called Lord Sikora. I come from the Kingdom of Ridley. This is my dragon familiar. I do not wish you harm. It appears that I have traveled too far. What has happened to the energy wall?"

"Yes! You have gone too far. You are over the border. I will provide you escort back to your kingdom, Lord Sikora. And what of that dragon? Is he dangerous?"

"Thank you for the escort. This is Snuffy. She has been with me most of my life. She guards me from all sorts. When the green of your meadow tickles her belly, she sneezes, and with that comes the flames. Flying becomes tiresome at her age."

Snuffy flaps her wings, gets off the ground a few feet, and lands on the arm of her trusted friend Lord Sikora. Lord Sikora grabs her and hangs on to her so she does not fall.

General Frank motions for Captain Mazelle to come over, leaving the princess to wait. "Escort the princess to the palace and inform the king of what has happened. Ride swiftly, as there could be other dangers in our midst now that the energy wall is gone."

Captain Mazelle nods and rides back to the princess. He informs her that there will be no more stops until they get back to the palace. The pair ride swiftly out of Deer Meadow.

General Frank escorts Lord Sikora and his little dragon Snuffy out of the Kingdom of Crystal City and back to his home, the Kingdom of Ridley.

Captain Mazelle and the princess come within sight of the stables. The princess breaks away from her guard and darts forward. Rankin has just walked out of the stables and sees the princess racing toward him. He waits and helps her off her horse.

"Rankin, we ran into a stranger in Deer Meadow. General Frank is escorting him back to his kingdom. I have to go and tell Father," says Princess Arabella. She dashes off to the palace to see her father.

Captain Mazelle arrives at the stables. He hands the basket and blanket to Rankin and gets off of his horse. The two men exchange looks, and Mazelle realizes that the princess has already informed

Rankin of what just took place in Deer Meadow. The two men talk as they take the horses into a stable.

Princess Arabella bounds up the stairs and through the crystal doors of the palace. She throws her jacket on a chair and goes looking for her father. She throws open the doors of the great room and there is her father, scribing. King Gerald looks up at the commotion and sees his daughter running toward him.

"What is wrong, Arabella?" asks King Gerald.

"Oh, Father, I had such a wonderful time with Prince Elgrin! I really want to get to know him. I want to see him again soon.

"And something happened on the way back from the gardenia field. We were in Deer Meadow, and there was a stranger standing there with a strange creature. I think General Frank called it a little dragon. He went to escort the stranger back to the Kingdom of Ridley."

King Gerald sits back in his chair and intently listens to his daughter recall the events of the last few hours. "Thank you, Arabella. I will speak with General Frank and find out what has happened. And yes, you may see your Prince Elgrin again, but in a few days. First we must find out what is happening at the borders. We must have an entry point and keep the rest of the borders secure, so we are not surprised by the strangers entering the kingdom."

Princess Arabella gives her father a quick embrace and kiss on the cheek. Then she leaves the great room and closes the doors behind her. She goes to find her mother, Queen Amelia, and her sister-in-law, Princess Likeria, to tell them the good news.

King Gerald has his arms locked behind his back. He paces back and forth, waiting for General Frank to come in.

With a shudder of the doors, General Frank and Captain Mazelle enter the great room. They bow to the king. King Gerald motions for the two guards to sit.

The conversation begins with General Frank telling the interested king of the happenings at Deer Meadow. "So we know that it won't be long before the kingdoms are flooded with strangers, causing much upset," says the king. "General Frank, get word to all kingdoms that the energy wall must be replaced with some sort of border—or wall, if you will—to protect each kingdom. We will also need to put a central border crossing at each connecting kingdom so we may monitor our visitors, for their safety and ours. The Kalliac requires that we live in peace. That, gentlemen, we shall do. We will be ready with all the borders and crossings in place by the time the great gala is upon us. We do not have much time.

"General Frank, it will also be your job to coordinate with the other kingdoms to get their borders and crossings built. Captain Mazelle, it will be your job to coordinate with our builders to get our border and crossing built. Prince Matthew will be instrumental in getting the Kingdom of Likeria to comply and to get that kingdom's border and crossing built as well. You have your orders. Now be off," commands King Gerald.

General Frank makes his orders known across all the kingdoms. Time is short, and the work must be done quickly. All kingdoms must finish before the night of the full moon. Everyone wants a peaceful world to live in. Not everyone is accepting of this integration, but all kings are aware of the consequences if they do not comply: the world will be destroyed in chaos. Even the likes of the kingdoms of Loki and Amari are willing to work to together to make a new world.

Prince Matthew and Princess Likeria return to the Kingdom of Likeria to help King Olaf with the building of the border and crossing.

Building goes on across the kingdoms, surprisingly with merriment and joy. Builders sing their building songs with builders from other kingdoms. Everyone seems eager for this peaceful new world. They share songs, stories, and even food. People welcome the new into their lives and kingdoms. King Gerald is happy with this process. The Kalliac will be pleased.

As time grows near to the grand gala, Prince Elgrin and Princess Arabella's courtship deepens. While on a picnic—this time in Crystal City, on the palace grounds, surrounded by huge rose bushes and flower gardens—Prince Elgrin makes it official. With permission already granted by King Gerald, the young prince proposes to an already happy princess. Princess Arabella of the Kingdom of Crystal City and Prince Elgrin of the Kingdom of Hagville will marry.

CHAPTER 55

The time has come. It is the day of the grand gala. Everyone in Crystal City has been helping to ready the grounds and the ballroom to welcome the kings of all the kingdoms. The palace staff are all a-hustle and a-bustle, decorating the grounds. They add gazebos and arches and bridges with flowers everywhere.

There is extra special news: Princess Arabella and Prince Elgrin will marry on these grounds. It will be a joyous occasion indeed.

The preparations in the ballroom go as planned. The tables and decorations are in place. The flowers begin to arrive. Other servants are loading carts with the finest china and silver.

Hours pass. The smells coming out of the royal kitchen are incredible. The two rats, Omar and Dee, keep sneaking into the kitchen to see if any crumbs of food have fallen. They eagerly snap these up and run back into the tunnels to gobble them up.

Other servants help the royal family with their garments. Princess Arabella has chosen a beautiful light blue dress and accessories. Her tiara and jewelry are all sparkling, as well as her shoes and shiny white long gloves. She is ready and waiting to see her prince. She has butterflies in her stomach. Ellie and Pooks play and giggle with her before she is summoned to join the rest of the royal family at the ballroom.

In the ballroom, they take their places. The guests will soon arrive. The servants stand at attention as well as the guards. Horn blowers announce the visiting royals as they arrive. Music is played in the background by the royal minstrels.

The first guests announced are King Olaf and Queen Alexandria of the Kingdom of Likeria. All bow, and they take their place beside King Gerald and Queen Amelia. The remaining royal guests will follow suit until a circle is made of royals.

The next to arrive are Prince Matthew and Princess Likeria from the Kingdom of Likeria. The horns sound again to introduce Lord Octavious, Lady Kane, and their son Prince Augustus of the Kingdom of Loki. With the next blow of the horns, the stranger from weeks earlier arrives: Lord Sikora and his familiar Snuffy from the Kingdom of Ridley. Next to arrive are Lord Taras and Lady Oleen of the Kingdom of Ghost Valley.

Princess Arabella lights up as she sees the next arrivals. With horns sounding, King Minos, Queen Hag, and Prince Elgrin of the Kingdom of Hagville enter and take their positions in circle. Prince Elgrin stands by Princess Arabella. They smile at each other with a sparkle in their eyes.

The horns announce Lord Teagan and Lady Robin of the Kingdom of Tercan Ridge. King Ivan and Queen Katerina of the Kingdom of Wolansia follow. King Ohtee and Queen Janee of the Kingdom of the Silent Springs bow and take their place in line. More and more guests arrive until finally, from the Kingdom of Amari, King Hegedus, Queen Seanna, and Prince Robertson arrive. Everyone has taken their place in the circle and greeted each other.

All of a sudden, the great doors of the ballroom are thrown open, and Sirus the bluebird swoops in and lands in the middle of the floor. Sirus transforms into The Kalliac. Standing tall and regal in her flowing robes, she extends her arms in greeting and bows her crystal and vine-crowned head to all the guests. The guests also bow and are in awe of Kalliac, having heard stories of this tall white-haired woman who commands great power over all the worlds.

"Greetings! I am The Kalliac. I have come to see the joining of the kingdoms on this most special day. I have seen the signs that all of the kingdoms are following through on the requests I have made since the energy wall disintegrated. I am pleased that you all comply.

It is necessary to create a world that is peaceful. The world can only exist in this way. You all have made great sacrifices to bring this peace about. Without these sacrifices, the kingdoms would be thrown into many moons of chaos and destruction, leading to the end of this world. You have taken steps to save this world. There is much more to do, but the integration has started," says a pleased Kalliac.

King Gerald takes a step forward, as does King Minos. King Gerald says, "Great Kalliac, something has just happened that is part of the integration. Prince Elgrin has proposed to my daughter, Princess Arabella, and she has accepted." He bows and steps back. King Minos bows and steps back as well.

"It is with honor that I ask Prince Elgrin and Princess Arabella to come and stand before me," says Kalliac.

Prince Elgrin takes the hand of Princess Arabella and walks to the center of the ballroom. They approach The Kalliac, bow, and stand before her. The Kalliac takes the left hand of each and places Princess Arabella's delicate, gloved hand on the top of Prince Elgrin's strong hand. Kalliac takes a piece of her flowing garment and gently wraps it around the clasped hands. All is silent.

Kalliac looks into the sky. Eyes closed, she breathes deeply and says words in an ancient language. The Kalliac makes signs in the air before her while continuing to speak. She opens her eyes and puts a hand on the abdomen of Princess Arabella. She leaves her hand a minute. Princess Arabella feels warmth spread throughout her whole body.

Kalliac removes her hand and removes the fabric from the couple's hands. She smiles and places her finger in the middle of the princess's forehead, making a sign. She makes the same sign on the forehead of the prince.

The Kalliac bows to the chosen ones. They bow and return to their places in the circle. Kalliac takes a few deep breaths and speaks once more. "I could not be more pleased at the progress you all have made during this integration. There will be many challenges, but as I have witnessed this day, you have proven you are worthy of